SEMBÈNE OUSMANE, born in
his living as a fisherman, ag
he then moved to Dakar and a
was drafted into the French ar
and Germany. After the war, he returned to Senegal, but with awakening political and literary ambitions he went to France and found work as a docker in Marseilles. He became trade-union leader of the dockers, and until Senegal's independence in 1960 was a member of the French communist Party.

Le Docker Noir, his semi-autobiographical, first novel, appeared in 1956, and reflects Ousmane's experiences in Marseilles. Since then, his literary output has been prolific, with *Oh Pays, mon Beau Peuple!*, *Les Bouts de Bois de Dieu*, *Voltaïque*, a collection of short stories, and *L'Harmattan* appearing in rapid succession. The latter opened up a new avenue in his career, prompting an invitation to study at the Moscow film school in 1964. A prize at the Venice film festival in 1973, for the film of his short story *Le Mandat* earned him an international reputation as a director. In 1973 the novel *Xala* was published, and made into a successful film. Ousmane's latest novel appeared in 1981 – a major, two-volume work, *Le Dernier de l'Empire*.

Heinemann's African Writers Series also includes the following works by Sembène Ousmane, in translation: *Les bouts de Bois de Dieu* as *God's Bits of Wood*; *Le Mandat suivi de Véhi Ciosane ou Blanche Genèse* as *The Money Order with White Genesis*, *Xala*, and *Le Dernier de l'Empire* as *The Last of the Empire*.

SEMBÈNE OUSMANE

BLACK DOCKER

TRANSLATED FROM THE FRENCH BY
ROS SCHWARTZ

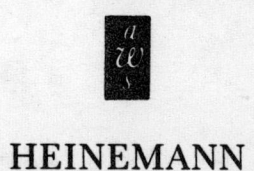

HEINEMANN

Heinemann International
A division of Heinemann Educational Books Ltd
Halley Court, Jordan Hill, Oxford OX2 8EJ

Heinemann Educational Books (Nigeria) Ltd
PMB 5205, Ibadan
Heinemann Kenya Ltd
Kijabe Street, PO Box 45314, Nairobi
Heinemann Educational Boleswa
PO Box 10103, Village Post Office, Gaborone, Botswana
Heinemann Educational Books Inc
70 Court Street, Portsmouth, New Hampshire, 03801, USA
Heinemann Educational Books (Caribbean) Ltd
175 Mountain View Avenue, Kingston 6, Jamaica

LONDON EDINBURGH MELBOURNE SYDNEY
AUCKLAND SINGAPORE MADRID

Le Docker Noir © Présence Africaine, Paris, 1973
Translation © Ros Schwartz, 1986
First published by Heinemann Educational Books Ltd.
in the African Writers Series in 1987
Reprinted 1989

British Library Cataloguing in Publication Data

Ousmane, Sembène
Black docker.—(African writers series).
I. Title II. Series III. Le docker
noire. *English*
843[F]   PQ3989.08

ISBN 0-435-90896-0
ISBN 0-435-90897-9 export pbk

Typeset by Activity Limited, Wiltshire, England.
Printed in Great Britain by
Cox & Wyman Ltd, Reading, Berkshire

CONTENTS

Part I

The Mother   1
Cath   9
The Clique   14
The Trial   18

Part II

The Story   41

Part III

The Letter   113

This book is dedicated to my mother,
although she cannot read.
Just knowing that she will run her
hands over it is enough to make me happy.

S.O.

Acknowledgements

The translator wishes to thank
Anne Wilson and Clive Wake
for their very helpful comments and criticism

PART I

THE MOTHER

Her face was wet with tears as she gazed after the ship which had just rounded the Almadies – 'The Breasts', Senegal's only mountain peaks. Mossy in some places, bare in others, their barrenness made them ridiculous. The savanna was broken up by knobbly, parasitic cacti. The baobabs looked neglected, like twigs shed from a broom. Nature had not gone out of her way to embellish this part of Africa. The liner cleaved through the waves. The reflections of the churning waters danced around the stern, like fleeting Will-o'-the-wisps. A large cloud engulfed the setting sun, filtering the reddish rays, tingeing the sky a deep rust. The sea pressed up against the heavens as far as the eye could see and the wind ruffled the surface of the water making thousands of shimmering scales. Endless sinuous wavelets rolled into each other; the foaming crests came and went, depositing their scum on the beach.

At her bare feet, crabs scuttled sideways across the sand. She could hear sounds from far off behind the dunes. Yaye Salimata had no more come to be alone, or to daydream, than she had to pay tribute to the setting sun. Close to fifty, her face was composed despite the turmoil inside her. Her faded eyes followed the 'smoke of the seas' which was going to the land of the *toubabs** and all she wanted was to go and join her son who was imprisoned in that place. She was the mother of five children. The eldest lived in Cayor with her husband, the youngest had left her one day to go to Europe. She lived with the rest of her family in Yoff, where she had watched so many ships go past that after a while they no longer interested her.

*Europeans.

The wonders of the white people did not affect her. She knew they could do anything: weren't they able to make those masses of iron float? They were in charge of everything, but hadn't God given the world all it needed? The presence of the whites did not bother her – she neither liked nor disliked them. But that was before. Now that they were holding her son, she hated them with all her heart, she cursed them. What was their country like? Big houses like in Dakar, trains which ran under the earth, children who did not live with their parents – so she had heard. 'Keep to your own, don't trust strangers, they only bring trouble.' Her son had not killed! He was not capable of slitting the throat of a sheep, the mere sight of blood made him ill. The *toubabs* had no heart otherwise they would have given her back her child. For some months now, men with cameras had been bombarding her with lights that they switched on even during the day. They asked her preposterous questions, they had taken her to the town, even the commissioner had joined in.

Far off in the distance, the trail of smoke imperceptibly vanished into the air. The floating mass continued lazily on its way until it was nothing but a black dot. The woman remained sitting on the sand, her tears flowing freely. Dusk caught her unawares and she went home. The children playing in the compound fell silent as she approached. She went and shut herself up in her room; a burning candle on a table lit the room with a feeble glow. The entire furniture consisted of an armchair without armrests, a bed covered with a white sheet and a basket in one corner out of which hung a brightly-coloured *pagne**. She lifted up the straw mattress made from old sacks and took out some newspapers.

In the latest paper bearing the previous day's date, the headlines read:

'THE TRIAL OF THE NEGRO DIAW FALLA,
MURDERER OF THE FAMOUS NOVELIST,
WILL TAKE PLACE IN THREE DAYS' TIME
AT THE SEINE ASSIZE COURT'

The words meant nothing to her for she could not decipher them,

*Rectangular piece of cloth worn round the body.

but in each newspaper, she saw a photograph of her child. His hair looked like a cornfield after a flood, his eyelids were swollen, his cheekbones prominent, his mouth would not close, his clothes were in tatters and his skin was the colour of burnt wood. She leaned closer to the flames until the edge of her kerchief almost caught alight. She moved away.

She could hardly recognize him from the picture. 'That hooligan isn't my son. They have killed him, and now they are tormenting me. Why did he have to go there, didn't he have everything he wanted here? Why did he abandon me? The *toubabs* are heartless, they are just like dogs, they have no shame, they kiss each other anywhere. My God, is it true that he is in prison? Ah! That woman, *dihanama** will not be hot enough for her; to hurt an old woman so. If I knew their cursed language, I would be able to read what they have written.' She was utterly confused. She dropped the newspaper, her white palms wandered over her cheeks and she pressed them to her eyes with all her strength, shaking her head heavily. She remained in this attitude for a long time before collapsing on the bed. She willed her imagination to show her the country of the *toubabs*, then she tried to supress the memories of her son's childhood, his first day at school, his shyness and his gentle manner. He was popular. 'It isn't possible, it isn't possible,' she said over and over again.

Throughout the whole affair, those three words comforted her. Her thinking became automatic from constantly asking herself the same question, turning it over and over in her mind. She clutched the sheets anxiously. Her kerchief slid off, uncovering her hair in which she had fastened a *greegree*† and a cowry shell. She writhed as if her insides were on fire. Her *pagne* came loose. 'Tomorrow, I'll go to Dakar, perhaps I'll find out something,' she said to herself.

The bus to Dakar was surrounded by passengers and vendors. The driver, aided by a youth, was stowing baskets of fruit and fish. In the east, the sky grew light as dawn broke. There were already many people there when Yaye Salimata arrived. All eyes turned towards her; she greeted them, addressing a few polite

*Hell.
†Amulet.

words to each one and then quietly waited until the driver ordered them on to the bus. They all knew each other. Her visit to the imperial town no longer aroused comment, everybody was aware of her frequent trips: news of the affair had gone all round the village. The rickety old bus moved off, jolting the occupants. Salimata's presence dampened the customary exuberance of the women fish vendors. The bus went through Ouakum at full speed. Among the passengers, tongues were wagging nineteen to the dozen as men and women exchanged the latest news – from the price of grain to the possibility of marriage between this girl and that boy.

A man in khaki was standing by the driver who asked him, 'So, what about this business in the Ivory Coast?'

'You know that we civil servants aren't allowed to discuss politics, but I will venture to say that according to yesterday's *Le Dakarois*, there were more than a hundred deaths.'

'It's a disgrace!'

'What do you expect? We must do as they say, the Whites are our masters. Those young greenhorns trying to stage a coup. Well, as far as I can see they deserve to get themselves killed. If you think the Dimbokro affair is weighing on people's consciences then you're mistaken.'

He shrugged.

The driver, heaving his bus into a higher gear, snapped at the civil servant. 'You want to know why young people aren't content? Well, I agree with them. People are being killed. Do you think that's right? Do you think they don't know what's going on? I was in the war and I've seen a thing or two.'

He stopped talking and beckoned to the other to come closer, whispering, 'You see Yaye Salimata? Her son is in France, seems he killed a woman, perhaps they're going to kill him too or send him to jail. He's only got one murder on his conscience, the white people have just massacred dozens of men and they won't even be tried. Nobody asks them to account for their behaviour.'

'You're a fool, my friend,' said the man in khaki. People turned to stare; he continued in French: 'You don't know the difference between politics and sadism. This character you're talking about – we know what he's like. Why did he go over there in the first place? To live off immoral earnings. Look at his poor mother, she looks half-dead. The law must punish fellows like that.'

The driver braked suddenly, the bus stopped and the three rows of benches serving as seats collided.

'Get off,' said the driver curtly, 'better impotence than the risk of fathering a creature like you!'

'Look, N'Doye, I'll lose my job if I'm late. You can't do this to me!'

'Get off or I'll split your skull open!'

A woman elbowed her way through to them and tried to settle matters. 'No, N'Doye, we've got a long way to go. I don't know what you're arguing about, but don't leave him here. You know what life's like for a civil servant,' she said with touching simplicity.

'I said, and I insist, he will get off my bus, and if you don't like it, you can get off too.'

'So, get off, God isn't dead, the Ouakam bus will be along soon,' said the woman turning to the dumbfounded state employee.

'You wait, I'll write in and complain that you refused to transport a civil servant to his place of work. You'll be sorry when they take away your old crock.'

The angry driver pushed him out, abusing him in French. 'You and your boss – I piss in your face. I bought this "old crock" as you call it with my own money.'

He sat down again and drove off, followed by the other's imploring eyes. N'Doye was known for his good humour and his tough character. On his return from Indo-China, he had set up as a bus driver, with his savings. He was available day and night. If people owed him money, he never asked for it in public, and for this discretion he was greatly respected. What was more, he would run errands, which his competitors refused to do. At the entrance to the town, several passengers alighted, including Salimata.

'What time are you planning to go home?' asked N'Doye.

'The first bus this afternoon.'

She walked along the two canals of la Gueule Tapée. The workers were already pouring into the European quarter. They walked in groups, talking as they went.

The women carried gourds balanced on their heads, children had school books tucked under their arms, adults hastened their steps and old people were bowed beneath the burden of their years. Cockerels were crowing from the wooden houses along the way. Only 'Mendel's Rest' was built in a different style. It had been built by a former master who was murdered by a fanatic.

Full of dread, the woman walked as if in a nightmare, overwhelmed by her thoughts. She turned the corner of 37th street, leaving behind the embankment to walk on sand. Here, the population was different; the roofs of the houses were tiled or made of zinc. She crossed the waste ground, skirting the refuse tip, and made her way towards a house with green walls. It was a well-kept bungalow with a stone basement. Salimata knocked on the verandah door and waited.

'Come in, Yaye Salimata,' invited a woman's drowsy voice. 'My husband is having his bath.'

The hall was like all the other rooms, with a black, yellow and green tiled floor. There were photographs on the walls. The furniture showed a preoccupation with durability rather than style. The woman who had greeted her disappeared into another room. After a while, a man tastefully dressed in native costume came into the room. He immediately enquired after her health.

'We were talking about you only yesterday. I've heard from the lawyer, he says he'll do everything within his power. We have to be realistic.

'Realistic.'

'I sympathize with your distress, but don't you see, there's nothing more we can do, believe me. We've hired a lawyer and he's costing me a lot of money.'

'Here's the coffee,' announced Boubacar's wife coming back into the room having tidied herself up. She placed the cups on the table.

Her husband, who was standing, picked up his cup.

'You understand, there's no need for alarm. I've consulted magistrates who tell me he has a chance of getting off. After all, he didn't do it on purpose. Drink your coffee.'

'I don't want anything. I think that if I went to Tougueul*,

*France.

the *toubabs* would take pity on me. He's not a bad child, you know he isn't. Who will be there to support him? I'm sure he's ill. You know what he's like, he's always catching infections and they say it's full of diseases over there.'

'I've been meaning to go there right from the start, but my work has prevented me. As for your going, it's out of the question. They have snow there, it's nothing like here. Don't worry, he'll be back. In my last letter, I sent money to the lawyer to buy books for him.'

'Yes, that's the only thing he liked, he knew a lot, they even said he knew more than they did. They arrested him out of spite, I'm sure he didn't do it.'

'That's what we have to prove. In any case, next week, we'll know the outcome. You must have the strength to be patient, otherwise you'll make yourself ill. Drink your coffee.'

'I am ill already, I cough blood.'

'What's this you're telling me?' shouted Boubacar.

'Can't you see her face?' broke in his wife. 'I didn't notice it earlier.'

'You'll come with me and see a doctor!'

'I'd rather die than have a white man touch me, and I know that if they find him guilty, I shan't get over it.'

'Do you know what you are saying? Now you're making matters even worse,' exclaimed Boubacar. 'You ill, him in prison. Are you coming with me now or aren't you?'

'No, there's no point. They're killing him and they're killing me.'

Boubacar, the eldest of the Diaw family, was a master builder for a private company. Although he was childless and lived alone with his wife, he still exercised his rights as head of the family.

'I also had a letter from Catherine. The baby is almost due. I want to adopt the child, what do you think?' he asked.

'Oh no! She's a *toubab*. They'll be the death of me.'

'I'm going. Are you coming with me or not? Well, I'll come up to Yoff on Sunday.'

'Don't do anything. You won't see me again. My heart aches. I'm going back now.'

The man left, disconcerted, not knowing how to comfort her. The two women remained without exchanging a word. Weary of the heavy silence, the mistress of the house busied herself with household chores, leaving Salimata to her turmoil. She too left without speaking. She decided to walk, her *ciawali** protecting her from the sun. Vehicles were coming at her from all sides. Villas under construction between Dakar and Ouakam were springing up like mushrooms. She was tired: she felt a strange anguish in her breast.

---

*A rectangular piece of cloth dyed various shades of indigo. Respectable women never venture out without their *ciawali* covering their head.

CATH

Like her future mother-in-law in Africa, Catherine in Marseilles was tormented by anxiety. The room she shared with her adoptive father was somewhat cramped. It was divided down the middle by a curtain which they drew at night. The walls were grimy with smoke from the stove. The furniture comprised two chairs, two beds, a stool and a set of odd saucepans hanging above the table. The only ventilation was from a window.

Catherine Siadem was fretting. She had lost hope. It was many long months since she had received any news. The correspondence she had recently begun with her fiancé's relatives was the only relief she could hope for. She was seven months pregnant, and her father plagued her continuously with his insults.

Since his imprisonment, Diaw and she had only exchanged a few letters. In his last letter, he had told her that his uncle was dealing with the situation, and that had given her a little hope. Diaw's arrest had affected her deeply: doubts had begun to creep into her mind as to the truthfulness of the young man's account of what had happened. She cut out all the articles about the case. The facts were contradictory. The newspapers had cast aside all scruples in their bid to outdo each other. Because Diaw was black, nothing was sacred.

Catherine took the press cuttings out of her bag. One article said:

'The negro murderer of the famous novelist has just been arrested. Since his atrocious crime, Diaw Falla has been holed up in a hotel room in the rue des Petites-Maries, protected by a positive arsenal. He stripped the young woman of her possessions, smashed her skull then took refuge in this hotel where he was tracked down by the police. This was not an easy task for the custodians of public safety who had to use great resourcefulness. As a precaution, there were two busloads of police officers, for the memory of the drama which recently cost a police officer his life is still fresh.

'Diaw Falla is well known in the black district, an area inhabited by pimps, theives and pickpockets. Local people describe him as a shady, lazy character. A docker by profession, he only turned up for work when he felt like it. Of average height, with a thick-set neck, his forehead is almost entirely concealed by his hair. He appears to be rather obtuse. His arms have an abnormal droop. He has the gait of a hunted animal. It is easy to imagine how the negro, in a frenzy of sexual passion, seized poor Ginette Tontisane and raped her, then banged her head against the edge of the table. Caught red-handed, he ran off, scattering bank notes all over the apartment. Diaw Falla has very round, muscular shoulders. He seems to withdraw into himself when spoken to, ready to spring, his eyes full of hatred and scorn. He is like a creature that has never been exposed to the influence of civilisation. He bears no resemblance to the big, harmless, naïve "Sambo", who is strong, smiling and so dear to the hearts of good Frenchmen.

'Diaw Falla comes from a good family in a little fishing village. He was brought up by his uncle, who taught him French. He did well at school compared with other Africans of his generation living in Marseilles. His mother, who cannot understand what made her son into a murderer, has fallen ill as a result. In the village of Yoff, he had a reputation for idleness and they say he set sail for Marseilles to satisfy his taste for crime and make his living as a pimp.

'Local shopkeepers are up in arms. They have circulated a petition in the area, protesting to the city councillors and demanding the expulsion of negroes and Arabs who live only by plunder. This district in the city centre is a den of wolves. No traveller arriving here dares set foot in the place.

Nearly all the assaults carried out in the city are the work of these men. What is more, they can be seen walking along the Cours de Belsunce, dressed in the latest fashion, with drain-pipe trousers and knee-length jackets, their hats pulled down over their eyes, annoying peaceful citizens. What can we expect from these creatures who are incapable of responding to progress, who call themselves sailors but are ignorant of the workers of modern machinery?

'Diaw denied the murder all day, claiming that he was the writer of the prize-winning book. Given the evidence, the law should take energetic and radical steps to enable us to sleep at nights.'

The girl screwed up the cutting and slipped her right hand inside the neck of her grey–green dress. She caressed the chain round her neck from which hung two tiny silver horns – a present from Diaw. For the three years they had been seeing each other, Diaw had worn that chain without ever explaining where it had come from. He had given it to her on her last visit. The memory of that occasion was more painful to Catherine than the weight of the child she could feel living and moving inside her.

She picked up another cutting. A photograph of Diaw, handcuffed, with a police inspector on either side, took up three quarters of the page. The journalist wrote:

'The negro docker, killer of the novelist Tontisane who won the Grand Prix for Literature, was interrogated this morning at police headquarters in the quai des Orfèvres, Paris. After twenty-four hours of interrogation, he still kept to his initial statement in which he claimed to be the real author of the prize-winning novel: *The Last Voyage of the Slave Ship Sirius*. It seems unlikely. The police are pursuing their inquiries. The victim was loved by all the local people. Before winning the Grand Prix, she had already written two novels, one on the life of country folk and the other on the Resistance. She was thirty-six years old. Her mother, a war widow, collapsed when she heard the dreadful news.

'The negro, who seems shy at first, is brighter than one

thinks. The total value of the theft is not yet known. We hope that for once, the law will not turn a blind eye.'

Catherine was unable to read the article to the end, she could not understand anything. The truth was buried. 'He'll be sentenced to death, that's certain. What will become of me?'

Old Malic Dramé burst into the room without knocking. He leaned his stick against the wall.

'Why aren't you at work?' he stammered.

'I had to go to the Social Security office.'

'Ah! Yes.' he grumbled. 'Do you think I'm going to keep you in idleness? You could have made the soup. Have I got to do everything in this place? You'll turn out like your mother. You're not even married and here you are, pregnant. You'll end up on the streets. I'd have done better to leave you among the savages.'

Catherine got to her feet to prepare lunch, her eyes full of tears. Her bad-tempered stepfather watched her.

'Don't cook pig, you bitch. Are you trying to kill me? Have you seen, that hooligan boyfriend of yours is being tried tomorrow. When I think that my cousin wants to marry you.'

'I'm not for sale, and I don't want to marry him.'

'Ah! Yes, we'll see about that.'

Malic struck her violently with the back of his hand, sending her reeling across the room.

'You'll do as I tell you, otherwise I'll kill you.'

'Yes, yes,' she replied, her voice strangled with sobs.

Satisfied, he resumed his seat on the bed. Old Malic had married Catherine's mother in the Caledonian Islands. Catherine had come to France as a small child with her mother. Her real father had been a white man who had died of malaria. During the war, Malic had joined the Free French forces in England, leaving his pregnant wife behind. She contracted angina, partly due to undernourishment, and died shortly after the Armistice. Then, Malic entrusted his own daughter's education to the nuns, while Catherine was taught to sew. Like many of his fellow-countrymen, whose pride was wounded daily by the press, the old man was irascible.

'I'm going out, and when I come back, I'll bring your future husband with me. I hope to God he still wants you and your bastard child!'

Malic's tongue was as sharp as his hand was quick to strike. In the colony, he was spoken of with fear.

'Leave,' said Catherine, 'I won't be here when you get back.' She had bruises on her neck and arms.

THE CLIQUE

'Mama's' laundry was at the crossroads of the rue des Dominicains and the rue des Petites-Maries.

During the summer, the doors were left open to relieve the constant heat of the furnaces. Two or three blacks were always chatting in the doorway. Towards the evening, when the factories came out, they were joined by others. 'Mama' was the nickname the Africans had given the owners of the laundry, not because of her age, but because of her kindness towards them. She must have been about fifty-five, her figure well preserved despite her long working hours. Whenever the young men had time on their hands, they would go and keep her company.

That evening, Mama was putting her feet up after a tiring day's work. She opened the latest edition of the newspaper. She had an emotional temperament and a tendency to reminisce about her youth and the values of bygone days. She dwelt on the 'news in brief' column for a long time. She was absorbed in the dreadful story of a child murderer and only looked up at the entrance of a newcomer. 'Hello Pipo,' she said, 'have you seen the papers? In my day, that sort of thing never happened. How can a child …?'

'You see, Mama,' said Pipo Alassane sitting down on the chair, 'it's not the child who's guilty, it's those people who promote sadism in order to undermine the moral strength of the generation they wish to control. It's the people who spread racism to maintain their system of profit, based on poverty and its most extreme consequences. They're the ones who go unpunished!'

'Perhaps you're right, but what's surprising is that it is the middle classes who are the most affected. They don't bring up their children properly. They are used to money and the cinema from infancy. I got married at the age of twenty and I never went out with anyone but my husband. Nowadays, wherever you go, you see girls and boys ...'

'Hello folks!'

'Paul! Have you seen today's paper?'

'You know, I've been here for ten years now, and not a day goes by without there being a murder in the papers. And some are carried out in the most horrific cold-blooded way. I'm thinking of that Englishman who strangled a woman, put her in acid to dissolve her body then continued his experiments on other women. Then there was that American who did in everyone who crossed his path and dumped the body in a dustbin. And do you remember that Frenchman who cut up his wife's body and left it in a basket at the railway station? What's amazing is that they're said to be 'mentally unstable'. Since when has a madman been known to dodge the law so skilfully? Then they have to be examined by a psychiatrist before being dragged before the courts, and if they're lucky, they'll get off lightly. That's their civilization for you. And so on and so forth. Primitive creatures have never committed such butchery. To be perfectly honest with you, this French nationality business is a lot of nonsense. Even if they cut off a piece of my flesh every day, I'd still insist I wasn't French.'

He spoke in a jocular tone. The others were no longer paying any attention to him.

'What's happening?' asked François coming in and finding the place unusually quiet.

'Look, here's Fatso. How's your family?'

'They're fine, Mama. Will you stand me a drink, Alassane?'

'I had a day off today.'

'With what you earn you should be able to put some aside instead of going off to the country every Sunday.'

'Don't be silly, what am I supposed to do with myself in town on public holidays? I prefer to go to the country. There at least I don't have to listen to idiotic prattle.'

They stared at Paul who was sitting on the table smoking a cigarette pretending not to hear or see anything that was going on.

'Well brother, is your head in the clouds?' asked François clapping him on the back.

'That's enough.'

'Ah! It's serious then,' François' pock-marked face puckered.

'Good evening everyone,' said Bouki in his deep, calm voice.

He was well groomed as usual.

The laundry owner stood up and said, 'I'm sorry, your shirts aren't ready. You'll have them tomorrow.'

'I don't need them. As I was on my way home, I thought I'd drop in and pick them up.'

He turned to François.

'Are you coming this evening?'

'You know I'm broke, Bouki. My kid's ill and there's my wife yelling at me all the time. But don't mind us, there's no reason why you shouldn't go ahead and drink.'

'Go to Pépé's and get the drinks.'

When they had all ordered, François went out. Although Bouki, the swindler, was a fellow African, he only resembled the others in colour. He was a slippery character and the others kept their distance from him. François returned with a loaded tray and took the task of serving the drinks very seriously.

'You know that Diaw's trial is tomorrow. They expect it to go on for three days,' announced Pipo.

'I haven't had a look at the papers yet. He hasn't got a hope of getting off; it's a shame,' said Sarr who was sitting alone, apart from the others.

'Here's the paper,' said Mama.

Paul took it and read aloud:

'The Court of Criminal Appeal has sent Diaw Falla before the Seine Assize Court for murder and attempted theft. The black man from Senegal, defended by Henri Riou, will plead unintentional homicide. The public prosecutor will be Michel Bréa. The Parisian jury will have a hard task with these two crack lawyers. Doubtless, the law will have the last word.'

He refolded the paper looking thoughtful.

'The novel has sold three thousand copies, neither he nor the woman is getting anything out of it. Only the publisher is making fabulous profits with the publicity over this business. There'll be a full house at the court.'

'I just can't understand what happened. He would only fight when his patience was stretched to the limit.'

'Please God let him be acquitted,' prayed Mama.

'We usually drink to his sucess; today, let's drink to his return among us.'

Bouki's words surprised them. Normally, he was indifferent to everything. He raised his glass, drained it in one gulp and made to leave.

When he was outside, they started gossiping about him.

'Well, would you believe it? But then he and Diaw do have one thing in common, they both like a fight. Crook that he is, Bouki is honest.'

'Hold on, François, someone's either a thief or they're not, and someone who makes a living from stealing isn't honest. Unless you can judge a man's honesty by his clothes. After all, smartness doesn't make an upright citizen.'

'Well, I don't understand a word of all that,' cried François.

'By the way, Mama, has a soldier been to see you by any chance?' asked Pipo.

'Oh yes, I forgot. He told me he'd come from Indo-China. Poor thing, he limps.'

'The "Priest" brought back more than four hundred wounded – the black soldiers are in a terrible state. And when they show them at the cinema, people feel sorry for them.'

'We'll be off, Mama, I can see you're nodding off,' said Paul.

'I'm sleepy. Goodnight, see you tomorrow boys.'

'See you tomorrow, Mama,' they rejoined making their way out.

THE TRIAL

Since the day he had been imprisoned, a real struggle had been taking place inside Diaw Falla. He reasoned and searched his heart to find a way of legitimizing his deed. His freedom depended on it. He could not rid himself of the obsession that he was guilty. He sought the strength to save himself from himself. If he tried to translate his thoughts into words, he remained tongue-tied.

Fresnes prison, where he was being detained, was silent at that time of night. The only sound was the echo of the gaolers' footsteps on the flagstones. Diaw had been allowed a cell to himself. In his solitude, he noted every sound, and distinguishing between the different footsteps helped him keep track of time. He could make out a noise coming from the ground floor: it was the four o'clock guards coming on duty. In two hours, he would be in court.

He had banished the days and nights from his mind. Sometimes, he did not even go for the walk in the prison quadrangle. Life no longer held any meaning, nor did sunrise, dusk, the stars, the moon, the clouds or the rain. He did not eat. The food he took was tasteless. With difficulty he swallowed what he was given to avoid getting stomach cramps. He would remain for hours on end with his eyes closed, searching in the recesses of his mind, contemplating his deed. He wanted to free himself, but in vain. He was beset by conflicting impulses.

Finally, they came to fetch him. He left the cell handcuffed between two *gendarmes*. He said nothing and took no interest in their conversation. In the prison van, each turn of the wheels brought his ordeal closer and made his heart beat twice as fast.

A crowd had gathered outside the court house. He was dragged out of the van. Flashlights went off from the press cameras. He remained impassive.

He walked down the corridors ahead of the armed men. They sat on a bench. Tight-lipped, he stared at his chains with distaste. He disliked his wrists.

If he hadn't had any, where would they have put the handcuffs? He was reminded of the slaves in his book. 'Why did I write it? Aren't I just like them?'

His lawyer came to see him. Maître Henri Riou was a small, elderly, balding man who was considered very active. His eyes bored into his adversaries, making them confused. He had a nervous habit of constantly smoothing his gown.

He reassured his client. 'Don't worry, son, answer all the questions as they come.'

'No, I'm not afraid.'

'Well, that's a good start. I'll be beside you all the time. I have to leave you now.'

Diaw was lying. He was so frightened that he would have preferred to return to his cell and await his sentence in the shadows. Riou left and he watched him disappear into the courtroom. An uneven murmur reached his ears. He began to think about those who were on the other side and about those who were in the same position as him. From the angle of double vision, it made him think of a corrida, the bull to be killed, or the matador. Then the roaring crowd crying for the kill. Either the man or the animal must die, without the spectators feeling a trace of pity. Neither is a murderer. If the matador kills, he becomes an idol. If the animal kills, it is terrible. And yet he could see himself digging until the end of his days to pay off that debt. A debt that would be passed on to all his descendants. The worst creditor was society, which always demanded its due, and, even when it was paid, never erased it.

He was suddenly filled with horror at his two escorts and heaved a weary sigh. He eyed them disdainfully then looked down, his jaw set. He spat. Their eyes met.

They removed his handcuffs and pushed him towards the door. Flanked by the two men, he stepped hesitantly across the threshold. The vast courtroom was too small to hold so many people. His heart was thumping so loudly that he could hear it above the hum of voices. The flashguns dazzled him, he closed his eyes. He was bombarded from all sides, plagued by the photographers.

In a burst of sudden anger, he sent a camera flying. This uncontrollable gesture created a stir among the reporters who came rushing over. The incident caused an uproar. He was escorted to the dock. His thoughts and his body were so tense that his lips were trembling. There was a pause, heavy with expectancy. To his left, the noise remained confused. He surreptitiously studied the crowd in the hope of spotting a friendly face: in vain. Nobody whose eye he could catch to exchange a hopeful look. They all looked more or less the same, not one black face. He withdrew into himself but remained on the alert. He was the focus of all eyes. Suddenly, a burning, choking liquid grabbed him in the stomach and throat. He started at the announcement 'Will the court please rise', spoken in a deep hoarse voice. Everybody rose. Diaw Falla felt his heart contract. Riou laid his white hand on his. The coldness of that hand sent a shiver running through him up to his brain. After the judge had taken his seat, they all sat down again.

Diaw Falla watched his lawyer who was chatting to a colleague with a heavy jaw and a sunken chin. He did not trust this man from the way he was staring at him. They both scribbled something on a scrap of paper which they then handed to the Clerk of the Court's assistant. The note was passed from hand to hand. Henri was talking, the four people on the bench were leaning down towards him, listening attentively. He wished he knew what they were talking about.

The court fell silent. The judge disposed of the preliminary formalities. Diaw Falla could hardly hear. He disliked all this formality, it was gibberish to him.

Was he not their prisoner? Why humiliate him by chanting all this clap-trap? It was all just a rhyme, his name and Ginette's. He clasped his knees. Everybody was listening. He studied the crowd one by one, at his leisure. Then he categorized them: 'Look, two young people among the jurors, at least, they look young. Perhaps they're friendly? I don't expect anything from them with their pasty faces.'

A murmur of amazement brought him back to reality. They had eyes for him alone. He muttered to himself: 'Now what have

I done?' His head in the clouds, he had lost track of what was going on. The judge pounded the bench, calling for order.

'Will the defendant rise,' he ordered.

The room was rectangular. The public was crammed on to benches separated from the lawyers by an aisle. The jury came in through the witnesses' entrance, the door on the right, and was placed in front of the dock, to the left.

The identity questions were dealt with swiftly, then the first witness was called. A woman appeared, darting fearful glances about her. After taking the oath, she stood gripping the witness box.

'Madame, was it you who discovered the body?' asked the judge.

'Yes.'

'Would you tell us how you came to discover the body?'

'Well,' she began, falteringly. 'It's as I told the police. In the evening, or rather that morning. Well, I was doing the cleaning. I do the stairs, they're clean. The gentleman on the fourth floor, he came down and said to me: "The young lady next door to me made a row last night." "Oh," I said to him, "well, she's been entertaining a lot since her book came out." But then she didn't come down in the morning to pick up her post and she didn't come in the evening either ... "Well," I said, "better go up and see," but I don't like going up to the other floors very much. Then I found her door half open. I looked in, to be on the safe side.'

The woman had raised her hand. It was her gestures as much as her language that made the public titter. She continued, 'There was no reply. I went into the room. I screamed: "My God, Holy Jesus and Mary." I called for help and the residents came. Someone phoned the police from there.'

'Have you seen this man before, that is, before the murder?'

'Oh yes! There are no Arabs or blacks in our area. The first time he came, I saw him looking at the plaque. When I told him there were none of his kind here, he said: "I know where I'm going," and without so much as a by your leave, he went inside. I was standing in the doorway.'

'How many times did he visit?'

'Often. Because there were residents who asked me: "Does that black man live here?" Once, I bumped into him on the stairs and he put his tongue out at me. Then he laughed like a madman. Another time, I followed him to find out where he was going.'

'You were in the know, you knew who he visited. Can you describe his relations with the victim, were they friendly or intimate?'

'I can't bring myself to believe they were intimate. Mademoiselle Ginette was honesty itself. If he claims otherwise, it's to give her a bad name.'

'Does the defence wish to ask any further questions?'

'No, Your Honour.'

The next witness was a proud-looking man. His recently cut hair was greying. He stood with an air of one who was used to this kind of scene. After the oath, he answered the ritual questions with assurance.

'Claude Martin, fifty years old, publisher.'

'Did your company publish *The Last Voyage of the Slave Ship Sirius*?'

'Yes,' nodded the witness.

'How did this manuscript come into your possession?'

'She brought it to me.'

'Who is "she"?' asked the judge.

'I mean Ginette. I had already published two books by her. She came to me with her latest one. I read the manuscript and was thrilled with it, so I went to see her and after discussing it, we came to an agreement concerning the terms of publication.'

'Did she tell you who the author was?'

'She said nothing to me on the subject. I assume she wrote it. After she won the Grand Prix, she said: "Martin, I've done something wrong, I'd like to make amends."'

'What kind of wrong?'

'That's all I know.'

'Have you seen the defendant before?'

'Yes, the previous evening, Ginette was with us in a café in Saint-Germain-des-Prés. When she saw the black man coming over to her, she became sullen. When we left the establishment, the man followed us.'

'How did the defendant behave?'

'He was one table away from us. He didn't take his eyes off Ginette. He looked very angry.'

'Was he worked up?'

'Exactly,' confirmed Martin.

The faces of the crowd were damp with perspiration. A journalist had removed his tie and was hiding behind his camera, afraid that he might be unsuitably dressed.

'One question, Your Honour,' interrupted the defence counsel. 'Can the witness tell us how he chooses the manuscripts he publishes?'

The judge turned to Martin. 'Did you hear the question?'

'We are a limited company. We have outside readers who advise us.'

'Why did you make an exception for the victim?'

'I ... er ... had known her for a long time.'

'Do you think that intelligence is the prerogative of one category of people?'

'No.'

'That it has anything to do with skin colour?'

'I do not know how to judge the behaviour of a black man.'

'So how could you tell that the defendant was worked up on the eve of the crime?'

The room was silent. The guard sitting by the door had a coughing fit and heads turned to look at him.

The publisher became flustered, 'I could see it in his eyes.'

Maître Riou sat down again.

'The gentlemen of the jury will take note.'

Diaw recognized the next witness, it was the police officer who had arrested him. His raincoat was filthy and the collar crumpled. He stiffly took the oath.

'Will you tell us how you came to identify the criminal?'

'We received the telephone call at about five o'clock. My colleague and I were put in charge of the inquiry. We noted that there had been a fight. The position of the body and the scattered banknotes left no doubt about that.

'According to the autopsy, the murder took place at about four o'clock in the morning. It could not have happened if the victim had not been perfectly familiar with her killer. After three days of patient searching, we found a letter from the defendant with his address on it. We lost no time in going to Marseilles and, with the help of the local police, he was arrested.

'During his interrogation, Diaw stuck to his statement: he went to see the victim and hit her, but only to reprimand her. According to information we have gathered, the defendant had a habit of getting into arguments.'

Maître Riou stood up. 'Your Honour, can the witness perhaps tell us how long the interrogation lasted?'

The sergeant replied uneasily.

'It's hard to say. There were several of us taking it in turns.'

'I take note. Did the defendant agree to sign the statement?'

'No.'

'Thank you. The gentlemen of the jury will draw their own conclusions!'

After hearing the police officer, the judge suspended the proceedings.

At two o'clock in the afternoon, there were more people in the public gallery. The ladies' colourful hats contrasted with the men's bare heads. They commented on the presence of various celebrities, pointing them out to each other. Reporters on the look-out for gossip went from group to group chatting and firing questions.

Diaw Falla scanned the crowd trying to spot his lawyer. At lunchtime, he had only eaten bread and fish. He had ended up having a conversation with his two guardian angels. Sometimes, he no longer paid attention to what was being said to him. He mulled over his ordeal.

'All this jargon is only to torment me. I've got to stay here, for three days, to satisfy their curiosity, like a newly-discovered animal from the Ark.'

'Ladies and gentlemen, please rise.'

Gradually, the noise died down. The fans were switched on because of the torrid heat. After Falla had sat down, he noticed that Riou's seat was still empty.

'And he certainly won't risk breaking a leg,' he mumbled for the benefit of the public prosecutor. Henri made a theatrical entrance. Shaking out his gown, he said:

'Please excuse me, Your Honour, my lateness is due to the arrival of a vital piece of information which I shall present to you at the appropriate moment.'

The remaining prosecution witnesses were called in turn. The first one of the afternoon was Doctor Copet, the expert in forensic medicine. He was in his sixties, with horn-rimmed spectacles perched on the end of his hook nose. He stood squarely in the witness box; his head was bare. He swore to tell the truth, the whole truth and nothing but the truth.

'Doctor, you wrote out the death certificate. What was the cause of death?' asked the judge.

'Death was caused by the head striking the corner of a piece of furniture, which led to a brain haemorrhage. The victim did not die instantly, but a few seconds later.'

'So when the murderer left her, she was still alive?'

'Yes, but no operation could have saved her. There was something else: the twisting of the arm caused the shoulder blade to be dislocated. There is reason to believe that the antagonist, in this case, wanted something which displeased the victim, and when she refused to give it to him, he hit her over the head.'

'In your opinion, was this act premeditated, or committed by accident?'

'Premeditation seems indisputable.'

'Thank you, doctor. Any questions, gentlemen?'

'No, Your Honour,' replied Riou, half standing.

The next witness was an elderly man with a row of medals on his chest. Despite his infirmity, he seemed quite spry. He swore, as they all did, not to lie.

'André Vellin, professor at the Faculty of Medicine.'

'You were asked to examine the mental condition of the defendant. What were your conclusions?'

'Diaw Falla shows no sign of any mental disturbance. There is absolutely no doubt that he is very intelligent. His feigned indifference indicates a superior character.'

'Do you have the impression that he is a sex maniac?'

'Among black people, that is natural, and especially when it is a question of a white woman. They are fascinated by the whiteness of their skin which is more attractive than that of negresses.'

'So, if Ginette Tontisane had refused to submit to him, he could have gone as far as murdering her?'

'Yes,' confirmed the professor.

Riou rose.

'Your Honour, when the witness asserts that black people are sex maniacs, can he specify in what ways their behaviour differs from that of white people?'

'Science has shown that coloured men suffer from psychoses when confronted with a white woman.'

'As far as we are concerned, it is a question of one individual, not of the whole group. What are your conclusions based on?'

'On science.'

'Is this man mad or is he not?'

'No.'

'I was sure of it. How then can you say that he is a sadist?'

'I did not say that.'

'You have just called him a sex maniac. Taking advantage of a woman is one thing, killing her is another.'

'The terms we are using differ.'

As tempers were frayed, the judge suspended the hearing. Half an hour later, they were all back in their seats. Diaw Falla was so frightened that everything inside him became blurred. He stood there in the dock, his hand on the rail, his nails trying to dig into the wood. That hurt, yet he preferred that pain to the one that he was expecting. His eyes swept the room when the judge questioned him:

'Diaw Falla, stand up.'

'What were your intentions when you left Marseilles?'

Diaw scraped his dry lips before speaking. 'I had no definite plans.'

'How could you travel so many miles without thinking about the purpose of your journey? What brought you to Paris?'

'I came for a book.'

'And when you saw Ginette, what were your intentions?'

'She stole from me, and I wanted her to make amends.'

'Why didn't you go to the police, that's what they are for?'

'*They* wouldn't have believed me.'

'And why not?'

'Because I'm a black!'

'There's no segregation here.'

'Perhaps not.'

'So you took justice into your own hands, instead of lodging a complaint? But when you saw Ginette that evening, were you angry?

'For what she had done to me, yes, I was. She pretended not to recognize me.'

'And did her behaviour with the men in the restaurant annoy you?'

'I was angry with her for what she had done, not for how she was behaving.'

'Were you a little jealous?'

'Why should I have been? She wasn't my wife.'

'How many times had you visited her home?'

'I've never counted.'

'Were you on fairly intimate terms?'

'It depends what you call intimate.'

'Did you sleep at her apartment?'

'Yes. I spent some nights there.'

'When she no longer wanted you, you preferred to kill her?'

'I never loved her.'

'So it's because of money? You wanted to blackmail her?'

'It was rather the opposite.'

'How much does a docker earn?'

'When I was working as one, 133 francs an hour.'*

'Do you know how many banknotes were on the floor?'

'No.'

'More than a hundred thousand francs.† Don't you like money?'

'When I earn it, yes. I'm not a gigolo!' He spoke vehemently. The gallery followed the duel keenly. Diaw said to himself 'Considering the situation I'm in, I've got nothing to lose.' His pulse rate was normal again.

'Answer either yes or no,' instructed the judge who continued, 'Do you like white people?'

'Do white people like black people?'

'You are here to answer, not to ask questions,' he thundered.

'When I am shown respect, I return it.'

'You ought to know that reciprocity is not a condition of love.

---

*Approximately two shillings (ten pence) an hour.
†About one hundred pounds.

Do you like white people?'

The black man hung his head. He did not know whether he should speak the truth or not. 'He's certainly out to get me,' he thought. Suddenly, his mind made up, he straightened up, consulted Henry with his eyes and spoke.

'If they consider me as a human being, the feeling is mutal, but if they do not, then I will be like them.'

'So you hate them?'

'Did you not just say that reciprocity is not a condition of love?'

'You claim,' said the judge, 'that you are the author of *The Slave Ship Sirius*? Can you cite a passage from the book? Any part you choose.'

At this request, Diaw rubbed his eyes so nervously that the whites became bloodshot. 'I'll try the last chapter.'

He paused briefly and began.

'At dawn, the sky was dark, as it had been at dusk: there was no horizon. The prow was engulfed by the mist. In this pea-soup fog, the slaves melted into the night. From the open hatch, despite the weather, the smell of carrion mixed with the stench of vomit and strong sweat – the rotting of dead bodies – rose up from the hold, which had been designed by the shipbuilders so that the chained slaves could stretch their limbs to stop them becoming numb. A sailor, if necessary, could climb down and walk freely between the prisoners. From within, groans could be heard. The woman who had been made pregnant by one of the crew was crying. Not for her child, nor for the unknown father, but for herself. The irons were cutting into her swollen ankles. The women and men were entwined in different positions and had been ill-nourished for days. They sailed on unaware of their destination.

All the different ethnic groups were represented there. There were those from the valley, who lived by the great river flowing from the land of the men veiled in black. There were those from the north, who had entered a pact of mutual assistance against the common enemy. Then there were those whose cheeks bore three scars, and those who spent their lives with their herds, protecting them from the wild beasts. There were some who were blacker in colour, tall and slim. There were those who had crossed the deep ditches to enter the forest and avoid the men with red ears, those who came from the great Bâbâ.

Others had such prominent cheekbones that they looked ill. There were those with hook noses who spoke in gutteral tones. Their huts had such low roofs that you had to crouch down to enter them. Then there were those with the pierced ears of the gold diggers; those who had been dazed by magic, their whole life consisting of working to fatten the herd, which would be sacrificed for the feast, for it was on this condition that they would be allowed to go and join their ancestors. There were those who, when they spoke, looked like dogs in the night. Those who lived in the rocks and buried their dead near the caves to shield them from their neighbours' hunger. Those who had never gone beyond their frontier, whose eyes were like two stars in the heavens. Those who had never seen cloth, only leaves, indifferent to sun and rain and to the caprices of the weather. Those whose origins one could not guess, whose language and customs were incomprehensible. The men who bought them made no distinction between them: they were unaware that not long ago, they lived a thousand leagues from each other, unaware, too, of the difference in their customs and beliefs. All these innocent creatures were assembled there, and the expression in their eyes said all that cannot be expressed in words.

The first of the slaves to climb out of the hold had managed to slip off his chains. Followed by dozens of others, he crawled towards the helm. The sailor on duty was strangled in silence.'

Diaw paused for a moment.

'The ship was divided in two. In the stern, the slaves, in the bows, the masters. Nobody steered it any longer, other than the wind which was rapidly growing stronger. As the day waned, the storm swelled. Eventually, the yard gave way. The sea unleashed its fury, lashing the vessel from all sides.

The slave ship was drifting. Water poured into the hatch, bring a horrible death to those who had not managed to throw off their chains. The sailors made one final attempt to seize the boat. The raging sea swept them overboard. The howling of the wind drowned any cries. The rain sliced like a knife. Soon, the sails were reduced to tatters, the masts smashed to pieces, water was seeping in everywhere. A dozen black and white bodies, assassinated by man or by the elements, were being tossed about in the wash.

In this fight against death, the 'civilised' had returned to their primitive instincts. They defended their lives with animal selfishness. They fought among themselves to gain a place on anything that floated, kicking away or stabbing anyone who tried to scramble up alongside them. A long wail could be heard mingling with that of the wind. They rounded their backs and clung to the boat like limpets as the waves engulfed them. They beseeched Mary and her Son to have mercy on them. For the first time since the beginning of their venture, they called on her. Their prayers aggravated nature. Others clung to the cabins and sections of mast, their faces pale with anguish.

Meanwhile, the blacks wailed and executed indescribable gestures to appease their god. They flung themselves into the water in the hope of reaching land. The blades rose up before crushing their heads against the hull of the vessel.

By now, the bridge was completely submerged. The conflict which divided black and white no longer seemed to exist. There was no more language, belief or difference in skin colour. They were all afraid, afraid of dying. In this fear, an invisible current flowed beween them. They were no longer antagonists, only the hurricane ruled. The thunder rumbled like laughter over their heads. Believers and magicians begged its mercy, it swirled them round as it pleased. Flashes of lightning streaked across the sky. The elements pursued their task, sea and sky, wind and rain assured the completion of their mission.

Wood and iron, white and ebony, live and dead, all was nothing but a void. Like a leaf caught in a whirlwind, they sank down into the abyss.

Thus died men who thought they were civilised, dragging down with them those who had not yet reached that stage. That was the journey of the last slave ship. *The Sirius*, reported lost with all hands in Nantes on December 4th, 1824.'

Nobody dared break the silence. The photographers were wondering whether they should capture Diaw on film. There was a heavy pause. People held their breath. Diaw breathed heavily, his skin glistening with perspiration.

'How long did it take you to learn that?' asked the judge.

Diaw Falla's eyes were nothing but a gleaming slit. His jaw was clamped tight and his muscles convulsed. He replied scornfully: 'I did not learn it in prison. I tell you, I wrote it, wrote it.'

There was a commotion and the judge suspended the hearing until the following day.

The next morning, after a good rest, Diaw Falla's thoughts were so clear that he studied those around him. Henri Riou was gesticulating, going from one person to another. Again, there was a large crowd. The defence had only called one witness, a half-caste black man, who walked falteringly. His suit was the latest style. From the waves in his hair, it was obvious he had spent a long time in front of the mirror.

He rapidly stated his identity. 'Sylla Djibril, thirty-five years old, artiste at the Folies Bergères,' and swore the oath.

'Would you tell us how the victim and Diaw Falla met each other?'

'Well! Diaw had come to see me in the Latin Quarter. He told me about the difficulties he had been having with publishers over his book. They asked him for exorbitant sums of money. I promised to help him, saying: "I know a girl – a woman – who moves in those circles. Perhaps she can help you." A few days later, I saw Ginette at the Montana, and I told her about Diaw's problem. It was she who suggested a meeting at the Petit Cluny on the boulevard Saint-Michel. A phone call, and Diaw was told about it. In the café, Diaw showed her his manuscript and Ginette was thrilled with it. She said to Diaw: "You must come over to my place where we can talk about it in peace." When I next saw Falla, he asked if he could trust her. I assured him that she was honesty itself. The following week, I met the pair of them at the Bal Nègre. They didn't mention the book to me again and I didn't ask any questions. When I saw him again, he said: "I'm going back to Marseilles, but I'll come back when my book's published." I even asked for a copy. But in spite of everything, there was still a nagging doubt. And when I saw Ginette's photo in the papers, for landing the Grand Prix, it never occurred to me that it was for *Sirius*. A friend lent it to me and I rushed over to her place. She was out. That's it.'

'Did you read the manuscript?'

'A few pages, when I went to Diaw's hotel.'

'Why didn't you make a statement to the police?'

'They never asked me.'

'What was your relationship to the victim?'

'We were freinds.'

'And to the defendant?'

'He's my brother.'

'What?'

'I mean we're from the same country.'

'But you are from Guinea!'

'Yes, but we're both African.'

'You say that he's the author of the book. Perhaps it isn't the same one?'

'There can't be any difference between the manuscript and the published text.'

'Are you accusing Ginette Tontisane?'

'You ask me to speak the truth, I am telling you what I know.'

'Did Diaw love Ginette?'

'I didn't ask him.'

'At the dance, how did they behave?'

'Like everybody else.'

'Were they not ... aroused?'

'I wasn't there to probe his state of mind.'

'So why are you here?'

'Because nobody will believe he wrote the book.'

'What about the crime?'

'Well, I don't know anything about that.'

After this evidence, the hearing was suspended for a few minutes. When it resumed, the prosecution was ready to make their closing speech. Diaw Falla felt a sudden flush come over his body, like when he had moved his victim's arm, like the nights he had spent awaiting arrest. Everything in him contracted in the grip of fear, dread of that man, who would not spare him. The Assistant Public Prosecutor's eyes made his blood run cold and that was enough to banish any hopes he had. He could guess what he was going to say. Very sure of himself, Bréa attacked:

'Gentlemen of the jury, there are indeed circumstances when a defendant may be granted the court's indulgence. In this case, I do not see any. A man travels hundreds of miles to carry out his wicked deed. And the defence will have you believe that it was not premeditated? Let us trace the course of the drama, and a clearer picture will emerge. Months earlier, Diaw had met Ginette Tontisane and endeavoured to become her lover. He wrote her a number of letters from Marseilles. The young woman grew weary of his assiduous attentions. Then he came to Paris to try and see her again. He found her in the company of two men. Cowardly and jealous, he dared not carry out his crime. What did he do? He watched her and stuck to her heels like her shadow. When the young woman returned home, what did she see? This monster. What happened then? We can imagine. He sprang at her like a wild beast, and the struggle began. Caught off guard by the sudden attack, she was unable to defend herself. Diaw, crazed with lust, overpowered her and took advantage of her.

'Then they heard footsteps. The poor child tried to break free and he grabbed her by the arm, which he twisted as if it were made of paper. He knew, yes, he knew she had money and that she had just won a literary prize.

'And the defence will have you believe that he did not plan his attack, that he did not commit murder, that it was an accident! Do not allow yourselves to be swayed by his composure, it was precisely that almost animal façade which deceived Ginette Tontisane.

'Let us see, what did he do after completing his sad mission? Did he go to the police? No, he is too crafty. Was he sorry? No, a creature like that has no heart, does not know the meaning of repentance. Nowhere in the whole of his body is there a scrap of compassion for his fellow creatures. We are civilized beings: we left the animal kingdom as soon as we were able to distinguish between good and evil. We are endowed with the ability to think, to reflect in complete safety. We have devised laws that have replaced slaughter. These laws enable us to respect feelings and human worth. I am applying for a life sentence because I am not cruel and neither are our laws.

'Let us go back to the defendant. When he returned to Marseilles, he resumed his past life, spending the money which burned his hands, and extorting large sums of money from girls. His past is not on trial? The snake only has to bite once! The concrete evidence we have heard reveals more eloquently than I can the details of his crime. The offence is so atrocious, so bestial, that it is truly worthy of its author, who has no cause to envy the wild beasts of his native jungle.'

He stopped his speech, mopped his brow and ran a finger between his collar and his neck. He looked up and slowly picked up again.

'What are the points in dispute? The charge clearly sets out the crime. The defence is trying, by I know not what means, to prove to you that Ginette's death was not premeditated. However, the defendant specifically travelled to Paris from Marseilles – why? "He was robbed," he says. But what are the police there for? If only science had been able to prove that he was mentally unbalanced! But no! He is as sane as the rest of us! All he lacks is human feelings. Justice must be done, for the sake of Ginette Tontisane's grief-stricken family, for the sake of society! Diaw Falla's crime holds our institutions up to ridicule. This monster claims to be the author of *The Slave Ship Sirius*! This insult to our literature is also an offence. The French literary world has suffered a terrible loss. Ginette Tontisane was one of our great writers. She fell like those who devoted their lives to the glory of France, carrying the torch of liberty and equality, like those who gave their lives to safeguard national independence. We regret this cruel loss, this great mind cut down on the threshold of glory. We must make amends, not only to the victim, but to our literature and to our civilization.'

Bréa's voice rang out. Diaw did not miss one word of his speech. He bit his lips. He hated himself, loathed those present.

From the moment he set eyes on him, he had found Bréa disagreeable, and just then, he grew more hideous with every minute. He imagined a statue of Justice, her club at her feet, her eye sockets hollow. She resembled a skeleton, her neck too long and her round face with its rigid nose. 'Yes, yes,' he replied to his lawyer who was talking to him. But he had not understood a word he was saying. The prosecution resumed his seat. There was an exaggerated commotion, journalists moving about, coughing, the ladies at the back crying. Faces dripped with perspiration and the heat made shirts stick to backs. Diaw Falla felt icy.

'Don't get upset. Nothing is lost yet,' said Riou, attempting to boost his morale.

The hearing was suspended for the afternoon on this second day of the proceedings.

During this last phase of verbal sparring, the courtroom was in a turmoil. The heat was already making itself felt with intensity. The previous day's newspapers giving an account of the trial were used as fans. Diaw did not even feel the interest which had obsessed him at the beginning. He was defeated, inwardly as well as outwardly. He admitted it to himself. All his movements had become automatic.

'We are listening,' the judge declared to Riou.

The lawyer, leaning forward over the bench, his hands joined as if in prayer, slowly looked up. The courtroom remained silent. 'Your Honour, gentlemen of the jury, it would have been easier for me to defend a hardened criminal than the man who stands before you today. In that case, I would have invoked my client's irresponsibility, the decline in moral standards or the cruelty of fate. But Diaw Falla on the contrary is our own victim!'

Murmurs of approval rippled through the audience.

Riou exclaimed, 'Yes, we are going to judge a man, while we alone are responsible. The law does not distinguish between human beings, but our hearts know these differences. My client's guilt seems proven simply through the colour of his skin. He is the beast capable of anything, the savage who drinks the blood of his victim. The accusation rests on the hatred stirred up by the press, which distorted the facts to make a greater impact on the public.

'We know that Ginette Tontisane came into possession of the manuscript. Diaw, weary of doing the rounds of publishers, ended up entrusting it to her. He returned to Marseilles to earn his living by the sweat of his brow. For several months, only a few letters were exchanged between him and the victim. Ginette wrote this sentence which proves that he was definitely the author of *The Slave Ship Sirius*. "I received your last letter. If you don't want your book to be published, tell me. I don't know why you distrust me."

'Why did he not turn to the law when he realised he had been duped? He did not think anyone would believe him because of his double inferiority complex, due to his race and his social position. However, although we may say that one individual is superior to another, we cannot do likewise for a race. Besides, the experts are now convinced that there was once a black civilisation which came down the Nile to Egypt and founded our civilisation.

'In the Middle Ages, the University of Timbuktu used to exchange professors with schools all over the world. So what happens to our supposed superiority? Throughout history, different races have taken turns to be dominant: only the ignorant can find proof of a particular prerogative in the present state of affairs. What can be more confused that the notion of race? No serious ethnologist will maintain that after centuries of emigration, conquests and intermixing, the peoples of Europe present the least evidence of purity. Racialism is only a form of hatred. It is through fear of being a victim of it that Diaw Falla was reluctant to take his grievance to the law. It is we who have endowed him with that fearful complex.

'Alongside our country, we have created a nation inhabited by black people to whom we have taught our way of life. We have told them that France is a welcoming place, that her inhabitants like them. These words seem derisive when they see what it is really like. Gradually, the bonds between France and Africa have become increasingly strained so that now they are almost at breaking point.

'Gentlemen of the jury, in Africa, there is an elderly woman who is dying, weeping over her son. Hand the mother back her child. Let us try and make good our mistakes. If you give Diaw Falla back his freedom, he will see that we are fair, he will know that our system of justice is merciful. And we will be able to say proudly, in hushed tones: "It was our verdict that made this man what he is." If you keep him in chains, his hatred for us will only increase, and with it, the hatred of a whole people. Let us act worthily, of ourselves, our country and our hearts.'

As Riou sat down, the court was in uproar. Diaw was transfigured, it seemed to him that his lawyer had expressed his own thoughts. He shook his hand, their eyes met.

'Has the defendant anything to add?' asked the judge.

Diaw shook his head, a lump in his throat. The jury withdrew to deliberate. The hearing was suspended.

In the dock, the two guards were chatting to each other. Diaw lay prostrate, his eyes closed.

He was reliving the chain of events that had brought him before the court. And the first image that came into his mind was the black quarter of Marseilles where the drama had begun.

PART II

THE STORY

As you walk down the main road, the rue des Dominicains, and enter the little Harlem of Marseilles, you will see the parish church of Saint-Théodore to your left. Many people still call it by the name given to it by the Franciscan monks: the church of the Récollet fathers.

A few yards away is an intersection where the rue des Petites-Maries leading to the station crosses the rue des Dominicains which continues down to the boulevard d'Athènes. The rue des Baignoires runs at right angles to the other two, making a triangle around a single building which forms the heart of the district. At the beginning of this century, the town of Marseilles counted only a dozen or so Africans. Gradually, their number increased. Preferring to live as a community, they gathered in groups in the square, place Victor July, in what was the old quarter, with its squalid, narrow, dead-end streets. During the Second World War, half the old quarter of Marseilles was destroyed. Some of the black community left for England, the others went further into the town. And when the hostilities drew to an end, their number swelled. Black people poured in from all sides, drawn by the vicissitudes of seafaring and life in general. United by a community spirit and mutual support, they formed this village. Most of them were experienced seamen, each one having sailed round the world at least twice.

In this little Africa in the south of France, all the countries, all the different ethnic groups were represented. In keeping with the customs of their native land, each territory had its own boundaries: the cafés. Prejudices and origins were often the subject of argument.

There were Sarakoles, the most numerous, for whom life would not be worth living if they could not go to sea. Talkative, loud and nonchalant, they were also the most conservative.

The Susus were wily, cunning and timorous, while the Malinkes were calm and ponderous. The Tukulors, descendants of the conqueror El Hadj Omar, were very dignified in their movements. The Mandiagues and the Dyolas were nicknamed 'the African Bretons' because of their love of wine. The warrior Bambaras, without whom the bravery of the African soldier would not be legendary, were also traders, tireless marchers, and above all magicians. They were feared by the other tribes because of the curses they were able to put on them from thousands of miles away. There were a few Dahomeens, calm and thoughtful, Martiniquans, Moors. Then there were the Wolofs, very sensitive, crafty and artful. Their origins were a bit of a mystery, descendants from a mixture of African peoples. They were known as 'the black Corsicans'. In their behaviour, they swung from one extreme to the other. They could be as gentle as a lamb or violent as a volcano.

Diaw Falla was a Wolof.

The young woman wearing mauve ballet shoes stretched up onto tiptoe. She scanned the crowd of passengers arriving in a medley of colour. A horde rushed towards her as she stood on platform three between two engines. There was something peaceful and soothing about the hissing of the steam belching out of the huge machines after the great clanging of their arrival.

On all sides people were hugging and kissing, overjoyed at coming home. The porters in their faded blue uniforms went to and fro, pushing their trolleys whose creaking was part of the general commotion, the shouts and calls. For the third time, the loudspeaker calmly blared over the heads of the crowd:

'Marseilles, ten minutes' stop.'

People rushed about, bumping into and walking past each other, taking no notice of the faceless voice.

'Mummy, are we in Marseilles?' asked a little girl whose mother was clasping her wrist.

'Yes, poppet,' the woman replied hurriedly as she made for the exit.

The air inside the station was hot and oppressive, made worse by the steam from the engines.

The young woman dropped her heels back on to the ground. She was dressed in a flimsy white print dress with a pattern of pink and green butterflies which seemed to be fluttering all around her body. She looked over in the direction of the exit where all the passengers were converging. Her thick black frizzy hair was tied back with a piece of cloth the same colour as her frock. Her skin was naturally burnished, her large eyes were framed by carefully-plucked eyebrows, her nose was slightly flat and her pointed chin made her face look longer. Catherine Siadem was radiant with all the splendour of her nineteen years. Once more, she looked in the direction of the train and delight soon dispelled her disappointment. Her pastel-painted lips parted slightly revealing the tips of two rows of even, white teeth. With feverish impatience, she raised her right arm and headed for the train. The man kissed her long and passionately as soon as they met. Then, with a childlike, mischievous cheerfulness, he pushed her away saying, 'You always keep your eyes open when I kiss you!'

'Oh! So you've only just noticed,' she exclaimed, 'three months in Paris has certainly changed you, old chap!'

'No it hasn't, old girl!'

He picked up his suitcase which he had put down on the platform and together they made their way towards the exit.

'Because of you I stayed in Lyons all night.'

'Half the night, my dear.'

'It makes no odds. All the same, I'm glad you're here. Ah! Dear old Marseilles!' he sighed.

They reached the massive steps. The man stopped for a moment, to contemplate the city. Before him was the boulevard d'Athènes where the cars crawled along on each other's tails. The pavements swarming with pedestrians and carpet vendors in an incessant coming and going were shaded by plane trees. Far away in the distance, the statue of the Holy Virgin, nicknamed the 'Bonne Mère', was bathed in sunshine. Behind the city, the mountains rose in a jagged line. The streets snaking between the buildings and into the distance looked like footpaths. Happy to be back in his adoptive town, he walked down the steps while she waited for him below.

'I'm so tired!' he said reaching the girl. 'Hello, Lady Africa,' he addressed the statue on his left.

'What's Paris like?' asked Catherine when he had caught up with her.

'Paris,' he repeated dreamily, 'is Paris, with the Seine and the Eiffel Tower.'

'What about your book?'

'I'll tell you all about it, but first you tell me about everything that's happened while I've been away.'

'Nothing much.'

'What about the others?'

The others were the blacks, his fellow countrymen. Diaw Falla was very concerned about his brothers, even though he was not a sailor. But he knew they were destitute.

'Shall we sit on the terrace of this café?' he suggested.

'Yes, but I haven't got long. I've got to go and earn my bread and butter.'

'I'm as tired as if I'd been working, perhaps even more so,' he said.

'When I've got time, I'll feel sorry for you. I've only had two weeks' holiday. I spent my time doing the washing, the mending and the scrubbing. You think you've got cause for complaint!'

They sat down. The young man ordered two drinks. Diaw Falla, a native of Yoff, a small town a few miles from Dakar, had only seen twenty-two summers. He was of medium height, with a mournful look about him. His skin was amber-black. His hair, frizzy as an unploughed field, covered half his forehead. His slanting eyes made him look as if he had Mongolian ancestry. His lower eyelids were well defined and taut and he had a small, flat nose. He had simple taste and wore a grey pepper-and-salt suit. Because of the heat, he had undone his tie and a silver chain from which hung two tiny silver horns peeped out from his open shirt.

'How is your father?' he asked.

'Still the same, he curses under his breath and says you're a good-for-nothing.'

'Who knows, he may be right.'

He drained his glass in one gulp and went on. 'If I'm successful, I'll talk to him.'

'And if you're not?'

'I've told you before, and I'll say it again. I can't get married while I'm a docker. That's no profession. How and where would we live? A hand to mouth existence in a hotel room? No, I don't want that.'

'Tell me you don't love me then, that you prefer visiting museums and churches. There are others like you, who do the same work, but it doesn't stop them from getting married. And I work too. That's not a valid reason.'

Diaw rested his elbows on the table and scratched his head as if he expected the right words to come out and convince her.

'You don't understand.'

'Go on, tell me I'm stupid.'

'Far from it, but try and understand me. You know me better than anyone else, but you understand me the least. Life isn't a novel, or a cinema screen. We're young, we throw ourselves into life like someone dying of thirst at the sight of a drop of water. In his haste, he crushes it and the illusion of that drop disappears, he can't see it any more. What's left for him? To die of thirst and remain lying on the ground. That is what happens when young people without a proper job go rushing into marriage. How many do you know who live in hovels in the most appalling conditions, and blame the whole of society? That kind of life is not for me. Now I've got an opportunity.'

'You've been saying that for nearly two years now, while my father's been going on and on at me because of you. If that was all, I'd be quite happy. But you don't love anybody, all you care about is your books.'

Out of habit, he drew his hand over his eyes and pressed them. He drew a deep breath and stretched out his legs, saying:

'What else can I say? You're right.'

'I don't want any of this "you're right" stuff. When you start saying I'm right, it means you don't want to continue the argument.'

'I've only just arrived.'

'No need to tell me,' she broke in angrily. 'I know that. Besides, I've got to go.'

She glanced at her wristwatch, stood up and walked away. She had gone a few steps when he called her back:

'Catherine!' She came back. He said, as if in apology, 'Don't be angry with me, will you? I'm going back to get my luggage and then I'm going home for a rest.'

'You need one, this behaviour isn't like you.'

'I'll come round to your place this evening, as I used to.'

She stood before him and ruffled his hair.

'You silly thing!' she cried.

She went off laughing. He gazed after her as she made her way towards la Canebière. 'If I'm successful, I'll marry her. She shouts at me, but underneath she wouldn't hurt a fly. What's more, she's got a good figure. A bit empty-headed perhaps, but that's no problem. And if her father won't consent, we'll just have to see,' he murmured to himself.

He paid for the drinks and went up the steps two at a time.

The taxi drew up and Diaw climbed out. He looked up, studying the façade of the dingy building. Some of the windows had panes missing. The wide open shutters swung on loose hinges. Freshly-washed laundry dripped on to the pavement. He shook his head discontentedly. The driver deposited the two trunks on the pavement.

'How much do I owe you?'

'Three hundred francs,' said the driver fiddling with the meter.

He was immediately surrounded by the local black community. He shook the outstretched hands. Diaw Falla enjoyed an excellent reputation and when he left for Paris to see to his own business, he had also been asked by the others to go and see the representatives of *France d'Outre Mer*, French from Overseas. They all awaited his return, hoping that he would bring good news. Their situation was growing worse day by day. Finding work had become impossible for them.

They fired questions at him.

'I shan't say anything until everyone is here.'

'Hey, you lot, let the poor thing have a rest. Thank God, you've come back to us safe and sound. We've waited years, what difference does one more night make?' philosophized one man who seemed to be the eldest. He spoke with authority. A black man came running up breathlessly, his hat pulled down over his ears.

All eyes turned inquiringly to him.

'Ousmane's dead!'

The black faces registered a deep emotion. The thick lips were parted.

'When did he die?' inquired Diaw.

'This morning. My brother's only just told me about it.'

'And who's dealing with it?'

'There are two men at the hospital. But now you're here.'

'Yes son,' said the old man, continuing where he had left off when the bad news had been announced. Placing his hand on Diaw's shoulder, he went on, 'You always dealt with those things. God will reward you.'

'But I'm not the only one.'

'We know that. You don't need to be old to be a guide.'

He stared long and hard at his brothers and then deferred to the old man.

'Right, well, I'll take my luggage up, then I'll go. Take care of the *marabout*.'*

Aided by his friends, he carried his belongings up to the third floor and left at once without washing.

He went to the hospital. The two comrades who were dealing with the formalities handed him the papers which he thrust into his pocket. They accompanied him to the morgue where coffins made of rough wood were lined up against each wall, waiting to be taken away. It was freezing cold inside and a faint musty smell hung in the air. You had to be accustomed to such visits not to feel sick. The first coffin he opened was empty. In the second lay a man whom he had known. His expression had changed. Diaw opened the lid wider. A trail of saliva ran from the corpse's mouth, staining the cotton wool which served as a pillow. Diaw took out his handkerchief and tied it over the dead man's face. After gazing at him for some time, he closed the lid, leaving him to his solitude. He left with his friends who had declined the invitation to see their comrade again for the last time.

He carefully studied the forms.

'You two go and take the collection lists round to all the cafés,' he said to his companions.

*Holy man.

'The funeral's the day after tomorrow,' said the man on his right.

'Yes, it is, since you're the ones who booked it. I'm going to the rue Trinquet to see the charity people.'

The tram dropped them in the rue de Rome and from there they walked to the black quarter.

Alone in his hotel room, he unpacked his suitcases. In one corner was an iron bed at the foot of which was a bidet and a washbasin. In the opposite corner was a wardrobe with only half the mirror remaining. Next to it was a table surrounded by a red curtain. On the oilcloth with scorch marks was a dusty oil stove. Near the door was another table piled with books, and there were two cane chairs. That was all the furniture.

The trunks were open. He bustled about tidying up. The window looked on to the rue des Petites-Maries. He could hear the noise from the street but it did not distract him. Finally, he stowed the cases on top of the wardrobe. Then he leaned out of the window and watched the main road. The echoes which reached his ears were amplified. 'There's a storm brewing,' he thought aloud. He heaved himself up and leaned further out to get a better view. As he had predicted, a fight broke out in a café. From his observation post, he could see the two antagonists. The cries and shouts of the onlookers had drawn the curious to their windows and they leaned out laughing with gusto.

'Get him!' he shouted. His encouragement was drowned in the general hubbub. The two fighters found themselves in the middle of the street. Diaw mimed the ducking and the punches as if he were in the fight. It lasted for a good fifteen minutes until the spectators decided to separate them. They were both covered in blood. Disappointed that the spectacle was over, he mumbled at the man who had just parted the fighters: 'I'll get you back for this.'

He stretched out on the bed and fell asleep.

The knocking on the door grew more insistant. He awoke and asked, 'Who's there?'

'It's me,' replied a man's voice.'

'Who? Come in,' he groaned, irritated at being dragged from his slumbers. He lit the lamp. 'Oh! It's you,' he said at the sight of his visitor.

He passed his tongue over his lips. The man sat down on the chair.

'When did you get back?'

'At one o'clock. Give me a smoke.'

The visitor offered him a packet of Gauloises. Diaw lit his cigarette and leaned back against the wall. Finally, he said:

'How are you, Paul?'

'Me? Oh! not bad. How was Paris?'

'Nothing much to tell. Only that you can have a good time there, and there are so many girls! I wonder what I'm doing here.'

'Ousmane ... when's the funeral?'

'The day after tomorrow at two thirty. I don't understand why I'm always the one who has to deal with these things. Can't you do it?'

'You're mad, I don't have anything to do with those from the other world. Just the sight of them is enough to make me dream about them at night, or rather give me nightmares.'

'When they're cold, they don't bite, you know. It's the living you should be afraid of, not the dead!'

'Each to his own job. I'm certainly no undertaker,' retorted Paul mockingly.

'So that's the way it is. Just you wait until another one kicks the bucket, you'll see.'

'No, you can go and tell him to dig his own grave, and you'll see to the rest.'

Diaw threw away his cigarette butt and wiped his hand across his face. Naked to the waist and armed with a face flannel, he washed his torso. His bones protruded under his skin.

'By the way, about Catherine, did you know that someone's cutting the ground from under your feet?' Paul asked insidiously.

The soap lathered on his black skin.

'And who is this new rival?'

'A relative of her father's. He comes from America and wants to marry her. He's even thinking of taking her to Soudan.'

'What does the old man say about that?'

'You know very well he's only out for himself. He's letting the fellow keep him. But for the moment, the kid won't have any of it.'

'Ah! I see why she was in such a state this afternoon.'

Diaw had finished. He was drying himself.

'Have you seen her then?' asked the visitor.

'Yes, she came to the station.'

'So she knew you were coming?'

'You ask too many questions, Paul.'

'O.K. Wait until the old man beats you with his stick on a street corner, you'll change your tune!'

'I'll treat him the same way as I treat the hundred-kilo sacks, I assure you. He's a bastard, and I don't want him for a father-in-law.'

'But you do want his daughter!'

'His adoptive daughter. His own is at school. He'll have his hands full with that one!'

'I believe you. All the same, she loves you too. As a brother of course, but the Sarakoles don't see it like that.'

'They're clodhoppers, yes, clodhoppers, a hopeless bunch.'

'François calls them "the foreigners", since they know they're called clodhoppers.'

'Good old François. Only he can think up names like that.'

'Now in his case, I'll gladly take care of the funeral.'

By now Diaw was dressed. They went out. In the street, the blacks were either sitting or standing around in knots, chatting in their own tongue. Soldiers roamed from bar to bar, seeking out the prostitutes who sold themselves 'the cheapest'. Here, everything could be haggled over. Some soldiers were urinating against the wall, heedless of the passers-by. A shrill whistle rent the night.

'You're bursting my eardrums,' said Paul digging his elbow into Diaw. He looked up and said: 'It'll serve you right if old Malic greets you with his stick, you'll pay for all those meetings with his daughter.'

'Yes, but right now I'm starving. Will you stand me a meal?'

'What next? I'll eat my hat if you ask me to. And I was counting on you to come to the cinema with me.'

'If I could afford to pay for you, I'd be on the way back to Senegal tomorrow,' joked Falla.

'May God hear you.'

'Amen.'

The restaurant they entered was a converted hotel room. The paint had long since peeled from the walls. The customers were crammed in – some were even standing, holding their plates, while others were seated. The air was thick with a strong smell mingling with that of the food. At the back, near the kitchen, there was a low door that had recently been carved out of the wall, above which was clumsily scrawled: 'WC'. Here, the menu never varied. Day in and day out, for the sum of a hundred francs, you were served a bowl of rice or couscous. The restaurant owner was also the cook and waiter. He was not the blackest of them all, but it would have been quite hard to find anyone darker than him.

On the other hand, his teeth were so white that they were reflected on his lips. He always had a toothpick in his mouth. Some people said he even slept with it. The two new arrivals had to wait until there was room to sit down.

'You haven't told me anything about your book?'

'I gave it to a woman who's very well known in publishing circles.'

'When's it coming out?'

'By the end of the year, so she says.'

Two customers left the table. As they sat down, Paul went on: 'You trust her. In your shoes, I'd be wary.'

'What can I do? I kept the manuscript for six weeks after my arrival in Paris, and if it had not been for Sylla, I'd have come back empty-handed. I saw several publishers and they asked me if I had any money.'

'Rice or couscous?' asked the owner.

'Rice. What about you, Paul?'

'Two platefuls, the same as brother Baba,' said Paul, going one better.'

'Do you think a book gets published just like that? The Parisians are a nasty lot. Everywhere the swine ask me the same question: "Have you written a book before?" as if you're born with printed pages in your hand!'

'How much did they ask you for?'

'More than a hundred and fifty thousand francs.'

His companion snorted in surprise. Baba returned with the

steaming rice, placed a bowl in front of each of them and took the cutlery from his apron pocket.

'Supposing you become famous, then you won't eat with us any more.'

'Don't be silly.'

'I know what I'm talking about. When you see me, you'll pretend you never knew me. Or you'll be more polite and refined, and behave like some of the others saying: "I say, I believe I've met you somewhere before ... where was it now? Where did I meet this ragamuffin?" And then, as if it had suddenly come back to you: "Oh yes! I remember, it was in Marseilles." And I, intimidated by your success, will hang my head saying, "Yes, Sir." You will lay your hand on my shoulder as if I were a child asking: "What can I do for you?"'

Paul mimicked the different accents of the upper and lower classes.

'Eat, your food's getting cold. Do you think I'm capable of ...?'

'When you're poor,' Paul interrupted, speaking in his normal voice, '... in poverty, the strength that raises you up makes you able to think big. Obsessed with reaching that goal, you keep telling yourself: "If I set foot on that ladder, it's to help those who are steeped in poverty." And you fight, you fight, to climb up. But once you're there, money, the name you carry, all that seemed taboo ... and all the things I shan't go into now, take such a hold of you that you forget your comrades in suffering.

'Because you are struggling to remain at the top, it takes twice as much effort as it did to get there in the first place. Then you know what you stand to lose and what awaits you. In your fear of slipping, you are prepared to stoop to the lowest depths. If necessary, you will crush a living body. All that so you will never have to eat that bowl of filthy rice again.'

He fell silent, and swallowed two spoonfuls of rice. He ate for a moment with his mouth open and wolfed down the half-chewed food – he had no molars left. Diaw had listened to him calmly, with bowed head. At last, he spoke.

'Do you think I'm capable of such cowardice?'

'If you look at it one way, it's not cowardice. You fight alone, nobody can blame you. But morally, it is betrayal, since you are abandoning your brothers, and it is in their name that you will have raised yourself up. How many are there who were like you, and who said the same thing? Now, they have forgotten. You've got one foot on the ladder and time will tell. Unfortunately, I'm not the only one who thinks like that.'

'You're partial to moral philosophy?'

'No, no, since I don't know how to meditate, but I envy you for being able to spend whole nights thinking and then work like a cart-horse during the day.'

Paul Sonko was a little taller than Diaw, with a light complexion. He was a Bambara. His Christian name was not a nickname, as was the case with some of his compatriots who gave themselves a French name in order to integrate better, so they thought, into the life of the metropolis, or into modern society. His name was the result of deep bonds of friendship. In his native country, French Sudan, now known as Mali, old Bacari Sonko, his father, had struck up a friendship with a *toubabou**, before Paul came into the world. The two men were close for years. They were so fond of each other that the local people called them *balo-dé* 'the foster brothers'. As a mark of his affection, Bacari promised to make Paul the godfather of his next son and, contrary to belief, that is why the young Bambara had been given that name.

'Wait for me, I shan't be long,' said Diaw standing up.

'You didn't kiss and cuddle enough in Paris, and now you're off again here. Shout loudly if the old man catches you and don't stay for ever!'

It was completely dark. On the corner of the rue des Dominicains, Diaw dived into a doorway. He imitated the cooing of a pigeon three times, then hid under the stairs. Catherine soon joined him. It was hard to see the pair of them in the dark.

'Is it true that Ousmane's dead? The old man says that you're taking care of the arrangements, as usual. To let me know you were back, he said: "Your undertaker's home."'

'Who's the fat swine who wants to marry you?'

'We'll talk about it tomorrow. I've got to go back up, he didn't go to the cinema.'

*The Bambara word for white man.

In the darkest corner, they pressed their bodies together passionately and kissed.

The bar where the Wolofs drank was in the rue Claude-Puget, a stone's throw from the old church of Saint-Martin which is now the police station. Police officers also frequented the café: police and Africans rubbed shoulders. The owner, Pierre, was a middle-aged man, very friendly to his 'Senegalese' as he called them. Diaw Falla was his favourite. His wife had a head for business. She would smile at all of them, sympathise with their woes and give them encouragement too. She would often act as their scribe. Janine, as she was called, got on particularly well with her husband's friend, with whom she could converse. Their frequent intimate discussions made the other customers gossip, but it did not bother her. When she spotted the black man coming through the door, she left the other customers leaning on the bar and went to greet him.

'Here's Pichounet!' she shouted to her husband in the back room.

Pierre came out at once. There were only three tables, the blacks were sprawled over them, quietly chatting or playing cards. 'Here you are, brother!' cried the owner.

'I'm not your brother and I don't like your missus giving me nicknames.'

'You are my brother. I was born during the day, and you at night,' retorted Pierre making everyone laugh.

Still pretending to be offended, Diaw flung himself at him.

They clasped hands and had a mock fight, disturbing the peaceful card players.

'They're children,' declared Janine.

'I assure you, one day, I'll knock him out for two weeks,' said Diaw in her direction.

'Then I'll take up with you?'

'Oh no!' yelled Diaw, going round the room shaking hands.

'What are you drinking?'

'Milk, as usual,' he replied going into the kitchen and sitting down beside his friend.

She brought him a glass of milk. He asked, 'Will you lend us your cellar for the meeting?'

'It needs cleaning. I haven't been down there since the last meeting.'

'Is Paul here yet?'

'He said he'd be back in ten minutes, but, like any self-respecting African, he'll be an hour late.'

Janine spoke from experience, and she laughed.

Diaw went back into the café, glass in hand. He addressed his compatriots:

'Isn't anyone going to help me clean the cellar?'

Several of them set to sweeping and arranging the chairs. They spread old newspapers on the table, which served as a rostrum. When everything was ready, discussion began. A few moments later, their comrades arrived, singly or in groups. About thirty of them were seated and the others crouched at their feet. The din of voices could be heard halfway up the stairs. Around Diaw had gathered the most representative of the tribes. They all knew he was back, but nobody knew what news he brought from Paris. Last, arrived Paul Sonko, who elbowed his way through the crowd and stood behind his comrade even though he was the unofficial representative.

'First of all, I greet you,' began Diaw. 'Before telling you my news, there's a more important matter. Our friend is dead. Everything has been dealt with and he will be buried tomorrow afternoon. A coach will come for you at two o'clock outside the cinema in the rue des Dominicains. The *marabout* has washed the body. There is one thing I object to: after the funeral, I don't see the need to go drinking and say, as some do, "we're drinking to him".'

'It's one of our customs,' interrupted a voice from the floor.

There were protests and murmurs of dissent. Everyone wanted to have his say. Diaw settled down comfortably, leaning his head on Paul's shoulder. He closed his eyes and brought his palm to his face. One by one, the voices died down.

He went on, 'Maybe, but our position does not allow us to carry on. To cover the cost of the funeral, we had to hold a collection. There's no need to fritter away the rest of the money. We could share it among those most in need rather than propping up the bars of the cafés. Anyone who wants to get drunk afterwards is free to do so, but not on this money. Winter's coming, we all know what a hard time it is. Every year, some of our number fall ill, and they expect our help. What should we do, pour alcohol down our throats or stick together?'

They all held their tongues. A chair was passed from hand to hand above their heads. Paul grabbed it and sat down to take notes. Nobody said a word about the rest of the collection money.

Diaw continued, 'I did my best in Paris. When I arrived, the members of Parliament were getting ready for their holidays. All the same, I managed to see most of them. They are aware of our plight. They know that there are shipping companies who don't want us on the pretext that we're incompetent. They talked about the possibility of repatriation, they said that those who want to go home to Africa will receive a sum of money on arrival. I asked if the Europeans who live over there will agree to their offer. It's not repatriation, it's more like repulsion. One of them told me it was for our own good. Then he added that we'd receive "a monthly allowance, from the social security or the welfare office". So then I asked him "Do you think we're in Marseilles to be supported by the state? It is humiliating when we're refused work and called lazy. We're prepared to prove our competence to anyone who wishes to employ us. And you won't lift a finger to help us." He left in a furious temper. I have to confess that I have brought no news from Paris to raise your hopes.'

'Should've beaten one of them up', shouted one brother getting to his feet.

Heads turned in his direction. Youssouph the fighter was well known. He wasn't a bad man but he was sharp and quick tempered. He was one of the men who had been involved in the brawl the day before. He had a swelling over his eye. There was a commotion of voices arguing. Only Paul and Diaw tried to conceal their inner turmoil. The latter observed the scene with a good-natured expression, his head in his hands.

Finally, they quietened down, at the insistence of an old man with white hair, the evening of whose life had crept up on him in Europe. He spoke in Sarakole. Someone else translated his words into Wolof.

'I arrived in France in 1901. At that time there were only three of us. The ships were driven by coal, and we were useful for pushing the wheelbarrows down into the hold. On the Red Sea and in the tropics, the whites died like flies. They would come and beg us to sail with such and such or such and such a company. I spent both wars at sea. At the end of the last one, we joined the Free French. I was a greaser, my feet sweated, but at that time, they didn't think my skin would stain the sheets, or that I was very dirty. And now they won't accept us. I've been at sea for thirty-five years, but I'm not entitled to a pension: even for that, I've got to become a naturalized Frenchman. And yet I've got a naval record that says I served as a Frenchman. After two wars and so many years at sea, I'm not entitled to unemployment pay. If I want help, I've got to beg for it.'

Tears ran down his cheeks. There was a lump in his throat, preventing him from finishing. A painful silence ensued. A young man stood up, a stern expression on his face. On his temples, two scars marked his origins. He spoke in French, in a gutteral voice.

'I joined the navy in '40. Paul was in the same year as me. That same year, we underwent our baptism of fire aboard the colonial despatch vessel, the *Bougainvillaea*, in the Ogooué estuary. The battle raged for five days, and finally, the captain surrendered – he was a Pétain supporter. We were kept penned in like prisoners, for two weeks. On the morning of November 9th, we signed on for a new mission with the Free French Overseas Forces. We had to go to London, on 15th December. There too, they were suspicious of us, they bombarded us with questions. In the end, we swore loyalty to France. Paul and I were posted on board the corvette *Etienne d'Orfèvre*. We were there in the Battle of the North Atlantic. And often, I saw more dead than you would believe possible – both black and white, their stomachs swollen, their flesh torn by the fish. In those days, there wasn't the difference between skin colours there is today. We called each other "brother", sleeping together and sharing the same spoon to eat with. And now, they reject us and call us incompetent! At what point are we Frenchmen? French unity is a dream, not a reality. Should we turn to the unions?'

'We don't need to go and see them; it's thanks to them we're in this mess in the first place! It's the unionized sailors who refuse to share cabins with us. You don't think the union representative is going to kick out his brother or his cousin for our sakes, do you? They take us for fools.'

'So,' the young man went on, 'we won't turn to them. And tomorrow, we'll go to the *Préfecture*!'

Some expressed disapproval of that, others agreed. They were all in an impasse, they did not know who to turn to. Events had overtaken them, they were groping about in the dark and poverty made them blinder. As they poured out their hearts, they did not understand that this paralysing poverty and unemployment controlled them. They did not know what the root of the problem was and they made their demands in a vacuum. Diaw Falla sympathized not out of political or patriotic motives, but out of solidarity. He had never felt so profoundly restricted. He had reached a dead end; he wanted to do something, but what? He could only give moral support, and in the present situation that did not count for much. He attempted to speak but several times something inside him refused. Finally, he resumed.

'I do not know of anyone who might support us. We have only ourselves to rely on. Let's stick together. We're going to need a lot of courage and patience to get over this bad patch.' He stopped speaking. The audience realized that he was not able to help them. Sonko rose heavily, rested his hands on the table and leaned forwards. His expression was very calm: he wore the grin of the ambitious.

'First of all, I want to tell you,' began the Bambara, 'that Diaw paid for his trip to Paris out of his own pocket. That should give us heart, we're not alone.'

'We're the only ones who are starving,' interrupted Youssouph again. 'And to cap it all, they say we're French.'

'Listen and let him finish,' intervened the doyen on Paul's behalf. The latter carried on, 'Let's stop arguing. We've got enough troubles as it is to make our lives a misery. Do we have to bicker like women over trifles? That's all I wanted to say. Does anyone have anything to add?'

Pipo Alassane slowly took his place. He had been the last to arrive and had preferred not to disturb anybody. His pipe, which usually accompanied him everywhere, hung from his lips. His gaze swept over the assembly.. He had been a sailor before becoming a docker. He was the only one who had been to union meetings. The others considered him as their politician. And yet he spoke quite simply:

'Do you think it is possible for you to get out of this situation? Do you think there'll be a special status for you? No, here you live in Europe and you should align yourselves with the workers, since you are a minority.' He paused, and went on, 'You will only get out of this rut when you have understood that you mustn't isolate yourselves. You must fight out in the open. What you have just said may be true. Out of the three hundred of us here, how many are in work? A fifth! You blame everything on the unions. Have you any concrete evidence that they don't want to have anything to do with us? Is it the union that refuses to give you work? There's another reason. You will continue to be treated as children until you try to understand what is happening around you. Don't bring your colour into it, accept your responsibilities, present and future. There is a solution and you refuse to see it. We are our own worst enemies!'

They filed out one at a time. The scraping of the chairs being dragged across the floor and voices making the odd comment drowned the last words of those who were answering back, who found Alassane's speech disgraceful. Paul and Diaw were left alone, asking each other the same question: 'What are we to do?'

There is no doubt that the most prestigious part of Marseilles is the Prado. The main thoroughfare is flanked by two symmetrical banks, planted with four rows of trees. The houses with ivy- and honeysuckle-covered walls try to outdo each other in elegance. The people who live in them are the flower of the city. The Lazare family lived opposite the statue of David – a reproduction of Michaelangelo's. Their villa overlooked the main avenue. Madame Lazare was a 'real lady'. Her only preoccupations were her wardrobe, attending previews and society life. She was wandering from one vast room to another in this house where she lived with her husband and daughter. It comprised six tastefully furnished rooms, with wide windows and pale pink curtains. There were vases of flowers everywhere.

She was pacing up and down in the drawing room, in a state of great agitation.

'Antoinette!' she called.

'Madame?' inquired the maid coming into the room.

'Are you sure nobody has telephoned?'

'No, madame, there have been no calls.'

'Very good,' interjected her employer sending her back to her duties.

Madame Lazare, left to herself once more, remained confused. She went to the telephone, picked up the receiver and then, undecided, she replaced it. She walked over to the window and stared blankly out to sea. Suddenly, she grabbed the receiver. Her hand shook as she dialled.

'Hello, is that you, doctor?' she asked in a sugary voice, concealing her emotion. 'This is Madame Lazare. She's already left, you say? Oh! I was worried to death. Thank you doctor. I hope I'll have the pleasure of your company soon?'

She put down the receiver and went out to the perron. At that time of day, the bathers came to make the most of the last days of summer.

Andrée Lazare had just boarded the tram from the Stock Exchange. She had not yet paid her fare. She had a vague look in her eyes and her face was distorted by the searing pain in her abdomen. The jolting of the vehicle made it worse. The conductor, watching her, felt sorry for her. He was ready to come to her assistance, she looked as though she was having difficulty keeping her balance. Andrée inhaled from a little phial she had taken out of her handbag to quell her wish to vomit. Her cheeks were pale and her hair dishevelled. From time to time, she sniffed. She was dressed in brown jersey and her high-heeled shoes made her look taller. She was twenty-two years old. The short ride seemed to last for ever. When the tram stopped on the avenue du Prado, she alighted, steadying herself for a moment on the rail. With every step, she felt the gnawing pain. She tensed, biting her lip as she walked. She sat down on a bench, overcome with giddiness. Several times, she tried to get to her feet, but she remained listless, unable to move. Finally, she stood up but the pain sent her reeling. She moved on, not willingly but instinctively. A child on roller-skates nearly sent her flying. The shock made her tense up and the expression on her face frightened him away. He turned round and stared from a distance. She cut across the drive, reached the cast-iron gate and pushed it open with difficulty.

'There you are Dédée. I was expecting you much sooner.'

Without a word, the young girl climbed the first two steps and lost her balance.

'Antoinette, Antoinette,' cried Madame Lazare, 'she's ill.'

'Oh! Holy Mother!' exclaimed the maid on seeing Andrèe stretched out on the ground.

Puffing and panting, they somehow managed to carry her to the divan in the drawing room. Petrified, the mother stared at the trail of blood staining the parquet floor. Her daughter lay unconscious, suffering from a haemorrhage. In a state of panic, Madame telephoned the doctor, who arrived half an hour later.

'What should we do?'

'I must stop her losing blood. Bring me some clean towels if you haven't any cotton wool.'

The girl writhed, tensing her limbs. The maid stood round-eyed in astonishment.

'Whatever is my husband doing? He's usually home by now. My God, don't let her die,' implored the mother.

'Madame, you know what lies in store for us if she dies. So there's no need to ...'

The doctor did not finish his sentence. He spoke in a fearful tone as he leaned over the patient.

The dented 'Frigate' stopped dead in the middle of the lawn. Lazare sulked, angrily cursing the stranger who had crashed into him. He was a short, bald man, and the roll of fat of his double chin sagged on to his shirt collar, almost concealing the knot in his tie. 'Ah! Honestly,' he said to himself, 'those maniacs deserve to lose their licences!' He burst into the drawing room. Antoinette was removing the bloodstains.

'Where's Madame?'

'She's coming, Monsieur. Mademoiselle is unwell.'

He strode across the room, and found himself face to face with his distressed wife.

'What's wrong with the child?'

'Nothing serious, a migraine,' she replied pushing him out of the way to prevent him from entering his daughter's room.

'Call Doctor André.'

'There's one with her at the moment. Anyway, it's nothing

serious, just a passing giddy spell,' she replied dabbing her forehead which was damp from perspiration.

'Do you know what! A hooligan in an old crock drove into the back of me. To think I've only just bought the damned car! And the worst part is, he wasn't insured. Ah! Those workmen!' He agitatedly rubbed his hands together. His wife was absorbed in her own thoughts, oblivious to her husband's presence.

The doctor joined them looking despondent.

'How is she?' asked the father.

Labouring over his words, he said, 'She may pull through, but I can't guarantee it. When your wife came to see me, I refused at first.'

'What on earth is all this about?' roared Lazare.

'Nothing, my dear. Dédée's going through a very difficult patch. Besides, you know she is. She's been like this for six months.'

'Listen,' he said turning ot the doctor, 'I want to know what's wrong with my daugher!'

'Very well, I'll tell you,' said Lazare's wife 'but don't shout like that. Dédée was pregnant. I made her have an abortion because of your position, and it turned out to be twins. You know you haven't been very popular since you've been expecting your Legion of Honour. Do you want this business to become public knowledge? It would ruin your career.'

This declaration reduced Lazare to a state of helplessness. He felt completely demoralized, negated, destroyed. He was unable to utter a word. The doctor stood watching him founder. There was a heavy silence. As if to shake himself, he drew himself up and shouted:

'If she dies, I'll have the pair of you locked up!'

The hearse lurched about, jolting the old driver. The heavy silence of the cemetery was broken only by the sound of the horse's hooves striking the cobblestones and the creaking of the axles. The beast hauled, head bowed, not bothering any more over today's occupant than it did over yesterday's. Nor did it care about the monuments adorned with inert angels. Flowers thrived around the mausoleum. Behind the hearse, came the procession of blacks. It was very simple, no wreaths, no trappings.

When they reached the top of the plateau, they skirted round the main path. The graves became smaller and less elaborate. Summer was on the wane and the poplars swayed in the strong north wind. The black marble slabs reflected the sun's rays.

The old man bumped about cursing the badly-maintained road. As the cart rattled along, he could hear the coffin banging against the sides. The silent troop followed behind, branded with a collective suffering. They walked falteringly, each footstep bringing them closer to their destination. This affected them more deeply than the news of the death. A few told their beads, others, who did not have a rosary, counted the verses on their fingers as they slowly recited them under their breath. In the Muslim section, on the other side of the dip, the wilting yellow grass drooped over the daisies. The blacks lifted down the coffin and placed it on trestles, lining up behind it. The *marabout* placed himself between them and the dead man, his head turned towards the east. From time to time, the man who was acting as priest raised his hand to his temples saying: 'God is great.' The others repeated his actions and words. The operation lasted a short time. Then, without the help of professional gravediggers, they lowered the body into the earth using ropes, trying not to bang it against the sides of the hole. The burial began. They carefully shovelled earth into the grave. As the mound grew, they silently worked faster. When the hole was filled, they crouched round it linking little fingers. With the same serenity as when they had arrived, they chanted the verses from the sacred book. Diaw Falla stood distributing cola nuts to the men as they left. All this was done with the same fatalism as in Africa.

Paul Sonko was standing next to François Sené. His face was pockmarked and he had a short neck. His jacket was taut across his tomach. Diaw soon joined him.

'How did he die?' asked François. His naïvety was endearing. Nobody answered his question.

'You haven't told me how he died,' he repeated.

'You've been told several times, it was the chest!'

'The chest,' he echoed, not understanding what the Bambara meant.

'Holy mother! Do you understand now?' cried Sonko gluing his lips to his companion's ear.

'Not so loud, you'll wake him up.'

'Ignorance is bliss.'

'Thank you,' he replied.

As they turned at the Saint-Loup crossroads, they took one long last look at the world of silence.

Formerly, it had been a lush park in the centre of the town. But alas, that was before the war. When the Germans had occupied the free zone, they had neglected the plants which soon died, then, later, the Americans had built barracks there. That was how the Stock Exchange Gardens had become a prison camp. Now there were monotonous ranks of tall apartment buildings. The cours Belsunce stretched away on the other side of the Chamber of Commerce, with its countless brasseries, street vendors and hawkers – it was quite a centre for traffickers. A twice-yearly fair is held on the wasteland, in spring and in autumn.

That particular Sunday, a colourfully-dressed crowd paraded up and down, jostling, elbowing and tramping backwards and forwards. People thronged past creating an indescribable uproar and turmoil. The roundabouts turned to the strains of the hurdy-gurdy. The dodgem cars crashed into each other, driven by those who enjoy living dangerously. Here, shooting ranges where you could test your skill, over there, a candy stall from which the smell of burnt sugar rose, mingling with the dust raised by the trampling feet. In the background, a doughnut vendor, crying his wares in his lusty southern dialect. The passers-by stared at him as if wondering how to interpret his words.

Shrieks and screams came from the direction of the big wheel, high above the heads of the crowds. It spun round to the refrains from popular songs. Amid the commotion, wallets danced in the pickpockets' deft fingers. The circus music was deafening. 'Don Juans' got up like film stars were busy striking up relationships. Homosexuals eagerly lay in wait for their prey. The whores, with clinging skirts, touted for customers. At a distance, the blacks stood chatting in a group outside the Ferréol café, with nothing but an occasional indifferent glance at the scene taking place before them. They spoke the most diverse mixture of languages. All their topics of conversation were related to home, to their wives and families or a hope they nurtured which collapsed the moment the dream became a reality. Sometimes one of them would put his hand in his pocket and bring out a letter he had read over and over again, his eyes wandering over the geometry of the words as if he wanted to absorb every syllable. It came from home and he would report the news to the others. And they would daydream again, about the betrothed or about the animals bought to celebrate an alliance. The only thing they did not forget was their village and their patch of land, for that was something nobody could take away from them.

'What time is it?' Diaw asked Paul for the third time.

'Time to buy a watch.'

'Fools have watches. I'm not being funny'.

Changing the subject, he asked the Bambara, 'By the way, what's become of Dédée?

Paul winced and was silent for a moment before answering.

'She didn't turn up for our last date. You know her mother made her have an abortion, but there were two little tadpoles in there. She had to go and see that bastard of a doctor.'

'But why did she go?'

'Reputation,' retorted Sonko.

Paul Sonko did not fret. He kept his troubles to himself. He did not believe in fate, but held society responsible for everything that could happen to a human being. Diaw knew him well, and that was why he chose not to pursue the subject. He left, after saying, 'See you later.' The Bambara watched him vanish into the exuberant crowd.

'I had given up hope, Master,' mocked Catherine at the sight of Diaw who had kept her waiting.

'Shut up! I don't want any nicknames.'

'Yes, yes, yes,' she hummed.

Everyone in the 'village' knew about the love affair, but they kept it secret from old Malic Dramé who did not want a Wolof as a son-in-law. The real reason was his fear that he would not be looked after according to African tradition if Diaw married his daughter. Catherine admired rather than loved the docker. He told her this thoughts. She knew he was full of good intentions and listened avidly to his theories.

They walked along the left bank of the Old Port. The boats with red and black hulls bobbed gently up and down. The women selling pistachio nuts took to their heels at the sound of 'Watch out! Police!'. The touts for the Château d'If hailed the passers-by. The whole of Provence was out in their Sunday best. People were shouting and gesticulating or eating pizza. The air was pungent with the smell of fish soup, mussels and the sea. Arm-in-arm, the couple headed lightheartedly towards Fort Saint-Jean. Outside the barracks, the *Caserne de la Légion*, the sentry paced up and down.

'When's your book coming out?'

'Around December perhaps. Why?'

'Do you believe …?'

'In what?' interrupted Diaw.

'No, you don't understand what I meant. Your brain goes too fast. Do you trust them?'

'We judge others by ourselves. To listen to you, anyone would think you'd written it!'

'No, I know very well you did. I also know what you had to put up with. Days and nights locked up like a madman. I prayed you wouldn't fall ill. I often thought of coming to see you but …'

'But what? Go on.'

'Since the day you slapped me, I didn't dare come and disturb you.'

The Pharo Garden was unlike anything else in the city. It adjoined the fort, looking out over the narrow estuary of the old harbour. The green lawns, walks, flowers and the School of Colonial Medicine were renowned throughout the town. Diaw led his companion to the monument to the shipwrecked.

'You've seen it a thousand times!' said Catherine

Diaw sat on the stone bench and gazed down at the town. A unique view spread before him. The distant droning tickled his ears. The rooftops seemed like a Lilliputian forest dwarfed by the surrounding hills. New buildings hid the sordid steets from view. In the cover of the little port, he could make out only moving shapes and colours.

He shifted his gaze to his world – the big port. It stretched for miles. The liners were resting, the cranes sadly stretched their long necks above the warehouses. In the distance, a high diving board imperceptibly shook its scaffolding while everything else was plunged in a ghostly silence. For today, he banished this vision of being a worker from his thoughts. 'Down there,' he said to himself, 'it's a slum.' Beyond the port, the tall, dark, forbidding chimneys belched black smoke over the slate rooftops coating them with soot. Today was a holiday, but not for them. The curved pier embraced the high tide, protecting the buildings. He drank his fill of the sight below. Everything interested him, everything touched him, leaving its trace on the mirror of his imagination. A wind blowing off the sea brought the fresh tang of the ocean. He muttered under his breath.

'It's one thing for you not to say anything at all, but when you start talking to yourself, there's something wrong,' said Catherine, standing watching him.

'I was thinking,' he said, as if to himself.

'What about?'

'About me.'

'Selfish. What shall we do? I'd like to go to the cinema.'

He got up. They walked slowly. From time to time the young man would stop to watch the seagulls vanish and reappear whirring between the pale blue of the firmament and the deep blue of the Mediterranean.

A canoe glided over the smooth surface like a swan.

'I hope you haven't missed anything.'

'I'm as poor as Job; if I go to the cinema, tomorrow I'll be begging my bread.'

'That's what you get for having a fling with the Parisian girls!'

'I want to live as I please.'

'What is living anyway? What is life?' she asked. Diaw believed himself capable of describing everything he could see. He could think, reflect and meditate, but to explain the meaning of life... He immersed himself in his thoughts, delving into the depths of his knowledge for an answer.

'Life,' he began, 'is food and the world a cooking pot. Each life is a helping and each person has a plate which they fill as they choose. We cook and season these dishes accordingly. For the food to be edible, everybody has to pull their weight. And to understand this life better, we have to preserve the flavour and be aware that we all need each other.'

'Do you think I'm good enough to be your other half?' asked Catherine.

'Don't be so impatient. I'm not complete enough myself to be able to spare a rib! Here's the bus, let's take it.'

They ran to catch the bus and in no time it dropped them off on the Canebière, the very heart of the town. It was more crowded than Babel. There were all sorts of different nationalities, from the blacks with their ebony-coloured skin to the Greenlander or the Siberian Muzhik. There were Chinese with their feline eyes, Incas, albino whites and half-castes. People from the most diverse social backgrounds seemed to converge here. From the middle classes to the blue-overalled workers, and from the pimps in their platform soles, the *demi-mondaines* and lottery-ticket vendors to the Arab carpet sellers. Young women of easy virtue mingled with puritanical society ladies. There were priests in their black cassocks, children and begging gypsies. This dense crowd swarmed everywhere, without colliding, lingering in front of shop windows, chatting and shouting animatedly.

The packed trams ran to and fro amid the drone of traffic, the horns, the beggar and the blind man whose accordion drew the passers-by. This was the main artery of Marseilles, and the stranger arriving for the first time can only marvel at the nonchalance of the southerners. At this hour on a Sunday evening, Marseilles looked like a scene from a Pagnol film.

'By the way, when are you going back to work?'

'Tomorrow.'

'You don't sound too thrilled about it!'

'You've hit the nail on the head for once. We should only do the things we enjoy, and then I'd gladly work.'

'That'd be lovely,' she agreed emphatically.

'I bet you'd choose to do nothing at all.'

'Nobody likes work, not even artists. People are just greedy.'

'Hello,' said Diaw.

'Who was that?' enquired Catherine.

'A friend and his wife. Which film are we going to see?'

Each tried to persuade the other: Catherine wanted to see a western, he a drama. They decided to toss, tails he won, heads Catherine did. It was heads.

He had stayed up very late and was terrified of oversleeping. For the last three months, he had been lying in later and later. But, as soon as the alarm rang, Diaw Falla wiggled his toes to shake off his sleepiness. He got up, stepping on the books that were scattered everywhere and stamped on the cigarette butts. To save time, he made some coffee while he washed. The shock of cold water on his skin revived him enough to enable him to get dressed without dawdling. He tidied his room a little and noticed that he was not in a bad mood. He felt young and vigorous. He looked on his day as an adventure. Before leaving, he scrawled a few words that were running round in his head.

He set off for work carrying his hook and his lunchbox. The autumnal grey sky promised a bright day. Men and women surged out of the neighbouring streets forming an endless procession along the avenues. Like Diaw, they were on their way to work. The older people walked slowly, the younger ones were more sprightly, chatting as they went. A rag-and-bone man was bowed under the weight of his load. A road-mender was spraying the tarmac. The dustcart collected the rubbish, the dustbins clanging noisily. In the place de la Joliette, there was a human tide. The quayside workers poured on to the esplanade by tram, bus and on foot. One side was lined with cafés and along the other was the goods station. Snack kiosks were wedged between the trees. People were calling and seeking each other out amid the chaos. The dockers were divided by a great misunderstanding: there were the veterans, who had been in the strike, men who knew their job, and who, to assert their rights, had unanimously voted to stop work. To thwart this decision, unemployed workers had been brought in.

They did not mingle, but clashed for no reason. They attacked each other with the testiness of wild animals, often at the slightest provocation. In every heart simmered an unhealthy passion looking for an outlet. Outwardly, they appeared to stick together, in work that sapped the vital strength from their muscles. In town, they discussed only the port and things related to it. Their language was crude: they heaped abuse on the supervisor, the employers and the foremen. The uncertainty of employment inflamed the abcess. It was always the same men who were hired, the same men who went home. The expressions on their faces reflected their inner discontent. Their skins were branded by the searing sun and dulled by the harsh weather which made deep furrows in their faces. Their hair was eaten away by bugs in the cereals. After years of this work, a man became a wreck, drained inside, nothing but an outer shell. Living in this hell, each year the docker takes another great stride towards his end. There were countless accidents. Mechanization had superseded their physical capacity, only a quarter of them toiled away maintaining the pace of the machines, replacing the output of the unemployed workers. It was the rivalry of bone against steel, a question of which was the stronger.

The equipment was treated better than the porters.

In the port, two shops had been converted into recruitment offices. Diaw and his friends came to the 'Joliette' and, more often than not, managed to get work. The first arrivals were already queuing in front of the windows to sign on for unemployment.

'Here comes the Parisian,' said Boulboul, as Diaw elbowed his way through.

'You've come just at the right time, fresh, fresh as a daisy,' said N'Gor, a Hercules of collossal strength. He was the foreman. He was a former boxer and people feared him. His long legs were bowed under the weight of his body. He grabbed Falla by the scruff of his neck.

'The bigger a man is the more stupid he is,' groaned Diaw in the giant's grip.

'Strength is a gift from God. I make mincement of little runts like you,' retorted the frenzied man swinging his massive arms in a circle.

'I say you're a bastard,' Boulboul answered back.

'Oh! I am, am I?' N'Gor's eyes flashed with anger. Boulboul retreated, bumping into other hopefuls who were trying to catch the attention of the foreman.

'A curse on you and your race!' shouted an Arab clutching his foot. 'You trod on my foot, and that's only the little toe!'

After this fruitless exchange, N'Gor rallied his workers as if holding a court-martial. 'To Mandrague. I don't want any latecomers, last one watch out,' threatened the boss.

'Come and have a drink,' Alassane suggested as they parted.

'No, I'm not like you Senegalese. Bunch of clowns,' cursed Boulboul, a native of Madagascar.

'Don't come then. Go back to your whores in the rue Thubaneau,' added Diaw sticking out his tongue. 'Go and get stuffed.'

When the sun had gone down and the day was well and truly over, the holds disgorged this human lava from their bowels. They walked with heavy step, hunched and broken with exhaustion. The damp smell of sweat rose from their bodies. Their faces shone with joy and there was a sparkle in their conversation: there was food for the family and a hot meal waiting for them.

Already, the next day preyed on their minds. Plagued by the question of where tomorrow's bread would come from, they knew neither the bliss of rest nor the pleasure of Sundays. The only ones to benefit from the dockers' conflict were the bosses. Work lasted from eight to ten hours and sometimes even longer. They would be made to start at any hour of the day. This exhaustion, accumulated over long months and years, killed their appetite and made them thirsty. And it took a few glasses of alcohol to soothe the burning in their stomachs, aggravating it at the same time.

The mistral had been blowing for several days. The leaves fluttered down, strewing the ground. The air remained damp under a dark, overcast sky. Everyone went out armed with an umbrella.

Paul Sonko paced up and down outside the villa which was guarded by two uniformed policemen. He was growing weary of being unable to gain entrance. The passers-by threw sidelong glances at the scene of the drama. None of the curious bystanders guessed that this black man was closely involved in the incident which had disrupted this quiet area. Nobody even took any notice of him. He walked up and down the avenue du Prado, avoiding the police who were questioning people.

In the end, he sank on to the bench where, a few weeks earlier, Andrée had sat. He opened the newspaper and read dolefully:

'ARREST OF OBSTETRICIAN, FOLLOWING ABORTION

The police have arrested gynaecologist Doctor Martin Lefèvre who performed an abortion in his surgery on Mademoiselle Andrée Lazare, aged 22, residing in Marseilles. She died the following day.
According to the forensic doctor, he made a first attempt six months ago. The girl's mother made her pay a second visit to the quack doctor even though the foetus was developing normally.
The father, who was not involved, has not been arrested.'

He let the newspaper slip from his hands. He had witnessed so many tragedies, there was so much suffering around him! While he sat there, motionless, he relived it all in his mind. He felt a certain sense of vindication that the back-street abortionist and his accomplice were in prison. He was not completely satisfied because her father was still at liberty.

The last time he had seen Dédée, she had told him that her mother would no more accept a bastard than she would a piccaninny and that she had to agree to do whatever was necessary to preserve her father's reputation.

Now that the girl was dead, his thoughts jangled inside his head, placing him at the heart of this appalling complicity.

'What did I answer? What did I do? Did I act for the best? Didn't I abandon her just when she needed me most? What agonies did she go through before falling into the clutches of that brute of a "butcher"? How she must have suffered! What pain she must have been in! Did she think of me before she died?'

As these grievances multiplied, he laid the responsibility at the door of society. All is false, laughter is artificial.

Paul was not a good thinker. For the time being, he considered himself satisfied, vowing he would keep coming back until he saw Lazare, the girl's father.

Winter had set in with its laments, its rains, the wind and the cold. The bare branches on the trees reached up towards the sky. But in winter, early fruit and vegetables from Algeria were plentiful. It was a godsend for the dockers. The pace of work exhausted Diaw Falla, his mind was growing feeble. He fled the company of his comrades and took refuge in silence. He struggled against himself, to stop himself from sinking in what he called 'the degeneracy of the times'. He had the choice between two personalities: the docker, who was just an animal being, but who lived and paid his rent, or the intellectual who could only survive in a climate of rest and freedom of thought. Subordination was unbearable to him. He spent hours thinking in front of a sheet of paper, but the mental deprivation resulting from his physical tiredness perturbed his nervous system. He was filled with disgust for his profession and began wondering if he could find something else. Then, he would pick up his hook, turn it round and round, running his forefinger over its sharp point and speak to it as though it were a living person. 'How many tonnes have you lifted? How many hours have you worked, in how many holds?' He would be overcome by headaches. Inside, he felt as if pins were being stuck into his marrow. To avoid seeing a doctor, he told himself that this tingling in his brain would pass.

His second book was about an African doctor. He resolved to live with him and, from then on, he would no longer be alone. The novel was set in the land of mysticism in Upper Volta, between Ouagadougou and Fadagourma. He had never set foot in these places, and appealed to Paul Sonko who knew that region. The latter, worn out with his own grief, was unable to give him what he needed, so he ordered a map of Africa and completed his research with a medicine manual on colonial illnesses. The idea was good. With tireless persistence, he threw himself into it body and soul. To soothe his headaches, he took two pills a day. It was not long before he was taking half a dozen. It was as much use as a poultice on a wooden leg. Sometimes, after work, having eaten his supper, he would wander through the town on long walks with no fixed destination. In the rain, the long, parallel tram lines gleamed like blades. The wet tarmac reflected the street lights. Dawn often caught him unawares: he would rush home, change his clothes and resume his work as a beast of burden.

There was a wide gulf between him and his companions. He would grunt a few words in answer to their questions. He did not have any 'friends' in the true sense of the word.

He had not seen Catherine for over a week. Her absence left a void in him, which he filled with his labours. Paul had miraculously found a ship and left. He had come to the docks to see Diaw on the eve of his departure.

Diaw went out alone, to follow better what he called his vocation. One day, he entered a wine cellar in the rue des Dominicains. He was filled with disgust. He studied the interior in minute detail. There were several people, either sitting or standing around the barrels serving as tables. They were of both sexes, black and white. The glasses or the bottle were passed from mouth to mouth, from thin lips to thick lips. In a corner, slumped a man as limp as a half-empty sack, his head lolling on to his stomach. Between his spread-eagled legs was a pool of vomit, a mixture of red and green. One of his feet was stained and there were splashes on his jacket. His big toe was poking out of his left shoe. The vile smell of the bar nauseated Diaw, forcing him to leave. This scene destroyed the pleasure of all the beauty he had seen. He meditated. 'Those foundering creatures are castaways, swept along by the ocean of time. Poor wretches, they cling to the bottle. You cannot go any lower, there is nothing worse. And yet, they enjoy it. What about me, what will be my destiny?'

He made his way to the Bar Puget, repeating over and over again: 'A happy old age is better than a happy childhood.'

'There you are!' cried Janine spotting him. 'You certainly make yourself scarce sometimes,' she added from behind the bar.

'Hello Pichounet!' a little elderly lady with greying hair called affectionately.

'Oh! Gran, I'm so pleased to see you. It's ages since I last saw you.'

'Since last time!' said Janine.

'It makes you sick, doesn't it Gran, you speak to one person and someone else answers!'

'Yes, love. The girl who let you slip through the net was right,' added the old woman. 'You're getting thin, you'll end up going mad locking yourself away like that.'

'Don't worry, Mama, there's still room in the lunatic asylum.'

'I've never set eyes on a black madman,' declared the café owner.

'Tell me, Pichounet, will you let me read your book?'

'I'll give you a signed copy; "To my mother, the white woman who has done more for me than the woman who brought me into the world. To this rock, who in the middle of my solitude, stopped the tentacles of vice." I don't think I can say more.'

'Yes love!'

'Give me a glass of milk, I'm going to wash my hands.'

As usual, the place was packed out with blacks playing their favourite card game, *belote*. He returned and drank his milk, a gulp at a time. As he was preparing to leave, Janine's mother asked him:

'Where are you going?'

The entire family loved Diaw. And Gran, as he nicknamed her, often invited him to spend Sundays with them. The Senegalese found this gesture extremely touching, but he always declined. After a great deal of thought he replied slowly to placate his adoptive mother:

'To ramble is to walk, to wander aimlessly, to walk for ever, trampling the grass underfoot and crushing the dewdrops. To admire the countryside stretching as far as the eye can see, to smell the fragrance of rosemary, thyme and wet earth, to watch the wild dance of the slender poppy stems in the wind. It's also watching the petals fade, hearing the birds and the cicadas sing until they drop. Watching the trees marry their shadows in the dusk, the Dantesque forms of the tree stumps, the stars appearing under the blanket of night. In the distance, over there, at the foot of the hill, the town, its lights like white buttons studding a lady's cloak. That's what you wanted to hear, isn't it Gran?'

'Yes!' acquiesced the elderly woman's translucent face. 'And where are you off to now?'

'I'm going to stroll around the stores and admire the displays of ladies' underwear. When you can no longer caress them, you have to do it with your eyes, don't you?'

'You're completely out of your mind.'

He shook his head and shut the door behind him.

The knocking on the door grew louder. Diaw was writing. On the other side, his visitor seemed determined to come in at all costs. He heaved a deep sigh and grumbled, 'Come in.'

Catherine pushed open the door. Her anger showed in her eyes, the whites flashed with fury. In an authoritative voice, she asked 'Have you thought of me?'

'My work has taken over my thoughts!'

'You're selfish. To think you're a stone's throw away and I can't even see you!'

'Don't stand there. I'll light the stove, it's cold in here.'

She settled herself on the bed. When the room had warmed up, she removed her coat saying, 'Yesterday, I was wondering how much room there was for me in your heart, after the museums and the churches.'

'The eternal question,' said Diaw going over to sit beside the girl. 'Don't spoil this moment. There are things that don't need to be said. What kills love is words. We play with them like marbles. You've got no more brains than a sparrow!'

Catherine watched the flames dance. The room smelled of burning paraffin. Diaw lay down. He had a habit of talking to himself. At that moment, he was thinking aloud.

'I'd like to have a wife. For no other reason but to know that someone was waiting for me, to share my spiritual suffering, to care for me. Yes, I'd like to experience that!'

'Would you want me as a partner? I'm good. Perhaps I fly off the handle a bit too easily?'

'You said it,' interrupted Diaw. 'Stroke my back for a start.'

'I've learned something!'

'Start stroking my back.'

She slipped her hand between his shirt and his skin. He relaxed at her touch.

'Alexandre Dumas had black blood in him!'

From the way she said it, he was not sure whether she was asking a question or whether she was stating it as a proud fact. He hesitated before replying to see if she would repeat it.

'You seem to think it's something to be proud of. In fact, people who see blood or skin colour as a source of pride are stupid! Between the donkey and the horse, there's the mule. They are both irreplaceable. It's no easier to harness a thoroughbred than it is to train a mule as a racehorse. One thing is certain, both are noble beasts in their own way. Don't take any notice of such silly notions. He was a great writer.'

'I heard everything you said but didn't understand a word of it. Guess how I managed to slip away and come here?'

'How?'

'I told the old man that I was going to the cinema with a girlfriend. She came to pick me up from the house. Why are you laughing?'

'At your cunning. It's not bad.'

She did not agree. He drew her towards him and switched off the light.

Not only was the work hard, but winter made the workers belligerent. The rain and wind froze their fingers and their ears felt as though they would split open. They kept their jackets on for the first shift. Fruit arrived in large quantities from the various corners of Africa. Diaw Falla's nerves were on edge from the combination of exhaustion and debilitation caused by overwork. His state of mind deteriorated daily. At the end of each day, he promised himself not to return the following day, and the following day, he was the first to arrive. Often undecided, he planned to return to Senegal but he was banking on the success of his book to make that possible. The months passed without any news from Paris. It preyed more and more on his mind.

It had been raining solidly for four days. Hoisting the loading pallets heavily laden with produce exhausted the men. On board, there was not even time to have a smoke. They had worked the day before in the rain, and today it was teeming down. The general dissatisfaction expressed itself in their way of doing and saying things. The eight men were just waiting for a chance to drop everything, but either because they were afraid they would find no other work, or because they feared the responsibility, nobody dared be the first to take the initiative. And yet they were all disappointed in each other. It was slow dynamite, a time bomb. At around ten o'clock, the weather was becoming increasingly unbearable, their clothes were soaked and water was streaming down their bodies. Some of the men were beginning to cough.

'Shit! I'm not working any more! Even if it means not getting paid. I'm going up,' declared Boulboul bitterly, heading for the hatch.

N'Gor saw him and came out of his shelter. Stepping between Boulboul and the ladder he ordered, 'Get back to your job.'

'Raise the net,' he called to Pipo Alassane, the chief hoist.

The Madagascan returned to his post, shouting curses in his dialect that would have killed a fly settling there. He was in the same team as Diaw. The latter, smarting from the steel cable, was swearing at his companions at the top of his voice. He began to climb up the ladder.

'Where are you going?' asked N'Gor.

'I'm not married to you! You can treat them like a bunch of idiots, but I'm getting out!'

'It's not up to us to stop first!' added the giant when he saw that nobody was touching the goods.

Diaw elbowed his way through the mass of Arabs on the bridge, herded together like sheep, and shouted to the workers on the quayside. They were all soaked. Then, back on the deck, he addressed the rest of the workers from the other holds. They all agreed with him. In the end, nobody on the boat was working. N'Gor, furious, grabbed him by the collar and Diaw whipped his hook out from his belt. 'Let me go or I'll disfigure you.'

'Do you want to make me lose my job?' asked N'Gor, raising his hand.

'What about you, do you want us to die? For the last two months, day and night without a break, always faster! Today it's raining, we're not even allowed to stop! Are *you* getting wet? Shit! We're not slaves!'

'Just you wait! I'll leave you to starve to death!' N'Gor threatened.

This provocation was too much for Diaw. He lunged. Pipo intervened. The passengers, the visitors and everybody else stared at them. The din reached the ears of another foreman, nicknamed 'Tomato' by the dockers because of his nose which was always ripe, summer and winter.

'What's going on?' he asked, on seeing that nobody was working. He gave orders, 'Back to your posts, the ship is to cast off at midday.'

The dockers exchanged glances, their faces sharp and furrowed, their caps pulled down. Diaw, who was calling the tune, did not support them. It was his word and he did not want to take it back.

'Nobody will work in the rain any more. After all, you don't own us!'

'Is he in your team?' questioned 'Tomato'.

N'Gor nodded.

'Well, don't hire him tomorrow.'

'I'm not your wife! Nobody will touch another crate today. You're trying to kill us. How many of our men are in hospital? Or with compensation for industrial injury? We've had to work thirty-five days in one month. Not to mention overtime. Damn anyone who touches a crate!'

'We'll see about that!' retorted the foreman as he left.

'Go and get whoever you like, even the good Lord. As long as it's raining, you'll have to manage without us!'

Diaw spoke, but he was afraid. The cold liquid running down his body testified to that and there was fear in his eyes. It was a matter of defending his self-esteem. He wondered where it would all lead. He felt like getting out of there. Almost at once, the governor arrived. He was as clean as the workers were dirty. A pearl held his tie in place, his hands were gloved. His gabardine overcoat was not sufficient protection from the rain so the foreman at his side held an umbrella.

'So you're the one who's forbidding the men to work?'

Falla knew him by sight, but they had never exchanged a word. His heart beat twice as fast. He answered nothing, his lips quivered.

'Go back to your places!' ordered the boss.

'In this rain, you'll be lucky!' retorted Pipo sharply.

His intervention carried weight. All knew that he was a union militant and a good one. In the last elections, he had stood as a delegate from his factory. He had not been elected because of the separatists.

'Come back here! Don't let him frighten you!' said Diaw.

'Just you wait! If you don't finish unloading the ship, I'll only pay you for the first shift. But if you finish the loading, I'll pay you and you can all go home.'

'Can we do as he says?' Diaw asked Alassane in Senegalese.

'No, he wants to own us.'

Diaw had regained his courage, a courage which came not from the heart but from the gut. It was like a ball expanding in a container which ended up filling it entirely. At first, the stakes had been purely personal, but now he was trying to defend the others. He knew nothing of labour legislation. The only thing he was certain of was that when he said 'no', it was 'no' to the bitter end. Alassane was his trump card.

'So, you're not going to finish?' repeated the boss.

'It's pelting down,' taunted Diaw.

'Right, call in the law. We'll see who's in charge here! And give me your number!'

The black's reply was to put out his tongue, which caused general mirth. The 'gentleman' with all his power had been humiliated. He scowled in his get-up. His authority was reduced to nothing before the will of all those men standing in a circle round him, championed by this puny creature.

In the first-class gangway, those sailing for the colonies talked to each other in loud voices. A lady dripping with jewels declared brazenly:

'What a cheek, they come here begging for a living and now they want to tell us what to do. Those communists deserve to hang, every single one of them!'

'What do you expect? We give the workers too much freedom. Their arrogance is equal only to their ignorance!' added the man beside her.

The bus stopped: riot police spilled out, armed to the teeth, as if they were heading for the front.

'What's the problem?' inquired the chief.

'This man here's stopping the others from working,' replied the governor.

The armed men had already deployed, ready to charge. Pipo, who had taken in every detail, stood by Diaw, holding his hook.

'Are you the union representative?' asked the lieutenant between gritted teeth.

Diaw looked about him. On every face he read the men's fear that the worst would happen. Their eyes were wild with indecision.

'Yes,' said Pipo, on his behalf.

'Yes, yes, he's the representative,' cried a thousand voices. At that moment, Diaw wished the earth would swallow him up. Alassane had said yes in his place. His short clay pipe hung from his lips.

'Are you the union representative? All right! Keep quiet, or else watch out!'

'Hold it, lads,' he said to his men.

'If any son of a bitch tries to lay a finger on you, he'll have me to deal with,' proclaimed a North African.

'Quiet!' ordered the guard, toying with his truncheon.

The strike was not confined to the one ship. The other two alongside were also affected.

'We're closing the holds,' yelled the bosun.

'Listen, I want a word with you,' said the governor grabbing Diaw by the shoulders.

He shook himself free. 'No, I don't go in for secrecy. Speak up so that my comrades can hear what you have to say to me.'

'It's time,' cried the foreman.

'Grub up, lads,' said Pipo looking at his watch. They trooped off like sheep to the pastures, their heads bowed and their trousers patched. The smell of damp clothing hung in the air. N'Gor conversed with the bosses, Diaw and Pipo brought up the rear.

'I didn't know you were such a good workman. Defending your profession,' said Pipo.

'That's enough!' interrupted Diaw. 'You know more about it than I do, and you let me get on with it. You're the one who should speak out. You're always hanging around the union.'

As they went out of the gate, he continued, 'I didn't do anything special. I admit I was even afraid.'

'So I noticed. Do you think I'd have deserted you? Well, I wouldn't. Do you remember the strike? The veterans were fighting against this infernal pace, the high cost of living and the war in Indo-China. Their struggle failed because of us, their demands weren't satisfied. You aspire to being a writer? You'll never be a good one until you defend a cause. You see, a writer must forge ahead, see things as they are, not be afraid of his ideas. We're the only ones who can defend ourselves. Thousands like you are suppressed. The secessionists divide us, you won't see a union delegate here, other than the CGT. It's a pity you can't see any further than the tip of your pen!'

When they reached la Joliette, they went to eat at the restaurant opposite the entrance. They only had fifteen minutes. They descended on the place like a swarm of insects. All those hungry mouths, shouting and yelling – the restaurant owner did not know whether he was coming or going. He was pushed and pulled in all directions. Plates were grabbed in mid-air. They tucked into their neighbour's order, forgetting what they themselves had asked for.

'There's the union rep!' chorused the men upon the arrival of Diaw and Pipo.

'That's enough, all of you!' said the latter.

They rushed to finish, chewing the food ravenously. N'Gor came in, his jaws clenched, his eye keen. The room froze at his appearance. He laid down the law through his Herculean strength. He was the Atlas of la Joliette.

'You won't be working with me any more. No foreman round here will take you, otherwise he'll have me to deal with. Do you all understand?'

He made a sweeping movement with his massive arms, encompassing the whole room. Diaw did not flinch. He restrained himself. The men had stopped eating.

'You son of a bitch,' continued N'Gor, 'I'll teach you to forget the taste of bread.'

Angered, Diaw sprang to his feet, gripped the fake marble table and with a sudden violent gesture sent it flying. It broke in two. There was a general stampede. Pieces of meat went sliding across the floor. Some grasped bottles of wine and gulped it down to relish the scene better.

'I say you're a … that you're a bastard, no need to be so colossal to be so stupid.'

N'Gor stamped his feet. His wide nostrils were quivering. His breath came in a whistle. He was on guard, his fists clenched so tight they looked as if they might burst. His bloodshot eyes flashed. He charged and threw a direct punch which the other dodged just in time. Diaw retreated, jumped on to a chair and planted himself firmly behind. He was holding his hook. He struck out into the air, up and down and from side ot side. The giant opened his arms.

The dockers had emptied the place and gathered in the doorway, enjoying the spectacle. Diaw cursed to provoke the giant further. N'Gor chased him. He clambered over the chairs, going from one to the other. With a quick reflex, he charged into his opponent head first and stuck to him like a leech. With his right hand, he dug his hook into N'Gor's buttocks. The foreman was bleeding profusely. Taking advantage of his condition, Diaw rained blows on him.

The audience had had enough. Pipo helped the proprietor to separate them. They had a hard job, Falla refused to let go. Blood was pouring from the big chief's nose.

'Just you wait,' he said, wiping his face with the back of his hand.

Diaw stood at a distance, keeping out of his reach.

'I'll have your hide first. This is just a taste of what's to come.'

'Come and put some disinfectant on,' advised Boulboul pulling the injured man away.

He was brutally swept aside and he fell to the ground.

'Oh! You won't be hearing from me,' replied the life and soul of the team.

Gradually, calm was restored. Comments were exchanged with relief. N'Gor went to have his wounds dressed. The entire team prepared to jump on him if, by chance, he should want to take his revenge. That evening, a group of them escorted Diaw back to his hotel.

Humiliated, N'Gor no longer openly threw his weight about. His patched up nose made him look like a clown. He was the laughing stock of the labour office. But he bore a grudge against Diaw, and did all he could to fight him again. Often, he would take it out on those who had nothing to do with it. Woe to anyone who laughed as he went by! A few days earlier, he had punched an Armenian in the mouth and broken his tooth.

Diaw did his best to keep out of his way, but he rarely found work. The fruit and vegetable season was coming to an end. He signed on for unemployment: his guaranteed salary was soon spent. Word soon went round among the foremen of la Joliette not to take him. And none of them dared have him among them. And there was no room among the veterans. His anger against N'Gor had subsided. He did not harbour resentment.

His life grew daily more miserable. He wandered throughout the night, seeking trucks that needed handling. The rent for his room had eaten into his savings. His attitude to things had become strange: when he had been part of the team, he had not needed to worry about his room. Now, he was obsessed with the idea that he would not be able to pay for it. Sometimes, he did not go down to the labour exchange. Getting up to find work depressed, irritated and exhausted him. On several occasions, he tried to go to the union, but deep down inside, he did not feel the need to do so. He had never set foot there before. What would he have said to them? He remembered Pipo's words and began to realise that there were hundreds like him, who did not earn their daily bread, not working a single day in the week, because they refused to resign themselves to licking the boots of the bosses and supervisors. In this period of depression, the supervisors controlled the foremen and the latter replaced the dockers. The tallymen also doubled up as dockers.

Diaw Falla only found a few moments' pleasure in what he was doing: the book he was writing. This double existence required strength and care. He envied his heroes: he could starve them and make them suffer, when he had a full stomach. But now he knew that life was a daily struggle. He learned to loathe the poets and painters who depicted only beauty, who celebrated the glory of spring, forgetting the bitterness of the cold. The birds aren't just decorative, neither are the flowers. 'Do you have to be naïve to be taken in?' he wondered. Sometimes, he walked Catherine to work. The girl was an assistant in a large clothes store in the rue Saint-Ferréol. She held an important place in his affections, and he treated her very gallantly.

That winter's day was as warm as summer. Outside the cafés, people basked in the sun like lizards. Diaw and Catherine made a wide detour to prolong their moment of intimacy. They arranged to meet in the boulevard de la Liberté. They walked side by side in silence. This habit of walking without exchanging a word annoyed the girl, and she was the first to break the silence.

'It's a nuisance that you can't find work!'

They turned into the rue de la Grande Armée. Diaw had not heard his companion. His eyes were riveted on the conical twin spires of the church of Saint-Vincent-de-Paul, topped by two crosses silhouetted against the sky. A tram hurtled down the hill, braking with a deafening squeal.

'The irritating thing about you,' she continued, 'is that you're as stubborn as a mule, you're worse than daddy. What on earth got into you, fighting like that? I suppose you're proud of yourself.'

'You can't understand.'

'Go on, say it, I'm stupid.'

'You're right.'

She struggled to find an answer as she gazed at the man. In the end, she restrained herself and was silent. They reached the place Stalingrad. Diaw held her elbow as they crossed the road.

'Any news from Paris?' she asked.

'Yes, I had a postcard which didn't say much. I hope I'll hear something before the spring!'

'Hasn't it occurred to you that she's going to cheat you? Let's sit down!'

They had reached la Canebière, opposite the church. They sat on the double bench. Two old men were making the most of the fine weather, warming themselves in the sun and quietly puffing away at their pipes. The sunshine filtered freely through the bare branches of the trees.

'Why are you so distrustful?'

Catherine removed her black gloves. Through the closed windows of the Lafitte bookshop, she could see the rows of books. This sight made her feel afraid. She drew closer to Diaw. At that precise moment, she felt the urge to hurt him. She slowly stretched, and regained her composure. As if in the grip of a sudden torpor, she spoke:

'This confidence of yours makes me feel very wary. If you become a famous writer, you'll leave me. I read in a book – I can't remember the title – that men of wit should only marry their equals. I'm neither beautiful nor brainy. I'm apprehensive about your book coming out, and at the same time I want it to, for your sake. But for myself, I don't want it. I feel desperate. I can see all my dreams crumbling.'

There was a tremor in her voice. Diaw listened to her, the sentences filtering through one word at a time. Beneath his tough workman's exterior, he was highly sensitive. She had chosen exactly the right way of touching him.

Then her face took on its usual expression, with her plaintive childlike air. Catherine went on, speaking with restraint.

'I have belonged to you. After weighing up the pros and the cons, I don't regret what I've done. When my father beats me, I put up with it. I comfort myself by thinking of you and I say to myself: "He'll get you out of this." Yes, I'm jealous, jealous like any other creature defending its possessions. I've hundreds of reasons for being angry with you, yet I always come back to you!'

She took his hand. He abandoned himself without responding. He did nothing to console her, although her silence was her way of demanding an answer.

'Brains and beauty – it's difficult to combine the two,' he said. 'It's true that your love is more refined than mine. My love for literature is strengthened by the love I have for you. You've seen me in poverty and we have loved each other. Tomorrow,' he stopped, shifted to a more comfortable position and gazed at the church, 'tomorrow, when my book comes out, even if it does bring me into contact with other people, what do you think they could want from me, those people? Nothing. It's easy to deceive others, but you can't lie to yourself. I understand you, but you don't often think. You just repeat the same thing over and over. Oh! I'm not criticizing you, it's your nature. You love, and you believe it's a weakness. Here, I live in an atmosphere of debauchery. I love you in my own way, with simplicity and with all the power of my feelings. Don't get it into your head that I'm only trying to prove my virility or that I need you to check my moments of weakness. I only knew three women before you,' he concluded as if to excuse himself.

Catherine Siadem toyed agitatedly with the hand she was holding. She went on:

'You mean a lot to me. I can't give you either intelligence or beauty, all I can offer is my undying love.'

Diaw, who had not shifted his gaze from the church spires, followed the flight of a pigeon whose shadow created patterns on the steps as it flew close to the ground.

'You've got a complex,' he said. 'Everybody's different. Don't fret, be yourself and not the way you'd like to be.'

He raised her chin with his forefinger. She nodded in agreement.

'Let's leave. It must be getting late.'

He put his arm round her waist and walked her to the shop.

The days went by without bringing any news. Diaw hoped to finish his second book that summer. Unable to find employment, he devoted himself to his writing. For the third and last time, the doctor and the sorcerer were face to face. It was a dramatic moment.

Falla paced up and down, smoking a cigarette, when suddenly there was a knock at the door. He said to himself 'If it's Catherine, I'll throw her out.'

'Come in,' he said as the knocking grew more insistent.

'Damn!' he snapped at the sight of his landlady.

'When are you going to pay me?' she asked.

She stood there, her pudgy arm resting on the back of the chair. Diaw Falla sat on the bed, his back against the wall, running his hands through his ruffled hair. He studied his 'landlady' as he ironically called her. He looked her up and down with disdain, taking in the lattice of varicose veins meandering over her calves and climbing towards her bruised knee caps. The woman's knees resembled malformed bowls. Despite her apron, her paunchy stomach stood out from the rest of her body. Two flabby breasts rested on it, ill-supported by her perennial bodice. Her head was attached to the rest of her body by a stocky neck and her neglected hair, with split ends, was growing thin. Two horizontal lines replaced her shaven eyebrows and there were crows' feet at the corners of her eyes, which were caked with bluish mascara. Her nose was her only good feature. Her lipstick went well over her upper lip and stained her cigarette.

When he had finished staring at her, Diaw closed his eyes muttering to himself, 'Could Juliette ever have made a man's heart beat faster? No.'

Irritated at being the object of such a study, Juliette lost her temper and shouted:

'Do you think I'm going to house you for nothing? I don't keep pimps. If you don't pay me, I'll confiscate your clothes. This is my hotel, not the Salvation Army!'

'Not only are you a monster, but you also insist on calling this brothel a hotel. You never give us any heating in winter and you come crying that I'm a month behind on my rent. To tell you the truth, I'm skint, and if I did have any money, I'd go and eat first. Do what you like, the cops are your friends and I can't pay you.'

She simpered affectedly, 'If Sir isn't happy here with us, would he kindly forgive us and go and stay at the Grand Hotel on the Canebière.'

Then suddenly, she let rip with all the vulgarity of women who are used to men. 'Get out of this brothel as you call it, but before you go, you'll pay me every penny you owe me or my name isn't Juliette. I've dealt with tougher nuts than you.'

'I bet you have,' retorted Falla, enjoying making her fume. 'Where I come from we say: "Beware of those you've known for a long time." I've been living in this brothel for three years and I've always paid and worked in order to do so. Whereas you ... anyway, how did you make your money?'

'By selling my arse,' she foamed.

'You said it! First the Germans, then the Americans, now the blacks. You'd get laid for a croissant. There was poor old Mamadou whom you cheated to make your business profitable!'

'You can't prove it! This is my place. Anyone who doesn't like it can just lump it!' she retorted leaving the room.

He slowly got to his feet and planted himself in front of her, bending his head down towards her.

'Before you go, let me get off my chest what I have to say. You are a brothel keeper through and through. No, no, I don't hate you. I despise you. Don't worry, I'll pay you somehow or other. My conscience would hate to be in debt to you. You may go.'

He held open the door for her. On the landing, their eyes met. Diaw slammed the door shut.

The following day, still without work, he resolved to sell one of his suits. None of his compatriots was able to come to his rescue.

It hurt him to part with clothing, for he remembered the long hours of toil, sacrifice and saving it had taken to buy, but he could think of no other solution. He went to the rue des Chapeliers. At that time in the afternoon, the street was a human tide, a dense sea of heads, wearing berets, *burnouses* or simply bare. There was a rich variety of costume: jellabas, the latest fashion in tunics. The Gallic, or Charlie Chaplin, moustache seemed to be compulsory. The walls were cracked, peeling and crumbling in places. Washing hung from every window. There was damp everywhere. Somewhere, under ground, there must have been burst pipes, and the water seeping between the paving stones washed piles of refuse towards the drains, which gave off a vile stench. There were two dead cats lying in the water in a state of decomposition. Ragged children were playing in the puddle.

On the pavement, the goods were displayed. There was everything, from snuff to gas cookers. The buyers came and went, bargaining. In this teeming street, all the different professions, honest and dishonest, rubbed shoulders.

The bars stood in a row, all blaring out the same music with its languourous, nostalgic melodies. Opium and hashish were freely available.

The blacks and the Arabs were almost one community, founded on the Koran. But deep down, the fear of mingling was stronger than their common belief. Diaw was arguing with the first buyer. He was a difficult customer and his patience ran out in the end.

'Hasma, salaam if you like, but don't make me waste my time.'

'My friend, I want it, your price – too high. I give you six thousand francs.'

'No, eight thousand or nothing,' said Diaw, taking back the suit.

'Ooh, my word of honour, I've only got seven thousand. I'm a Muslim like you. *Valahi, Allahrabi*, I want it,' said the Arab, taking the suit from him.

'Of all the... go on then. To think it cost me twenty-two thousand francs to have it made.'

The North African paid up at once and vanished into the throng, while Diaw returned home.

The hotel office doubled as a kitchen and drinks were served there. He found a few whores and a man who seemed completely at home ensconced in an armchair with his feet up on a chair.

Diaw entered with a frosty expression and silently deposited the money on the table, then turned to the owner:

'Here's four thosand francs. You'll just have to wait for the rest. And what's more, I don't like you going into my room when I'm out. Cleaning is done in the morning.'

Juliette was amazed at his tone of voice and his attitude in front of the girls.

'Buy us a drink,' asked one of the women.

'I eat pork, but I don't keep pigs!'

The man rose, his hair was plastered down. He was as thin as Diaw but taller.

'Where are your manners?' he said.

'Shut up! I'm not talking to you but to Juliette, your wife and mother-in-law.'

As he said that, he drew back his left foot.

'Watch your language, you little runt.'

The words were not out of his mouth before Diaw butted him and knocked him over. The panic-stricken women scattered screaming. The office was turned upside-down.

He straddled the man, pinning his arms down with his knees and beating him.

'He'll kill him!' screamed Juliette, calling for help.

In the grip of a violent rage, Diaw pummelled his victim. 'You bastard! I don't like your sort!'

As he spoke, he struck from the right, from the left, from the left and from the right. His victim's head lolled from side to side with each punch.

The room soon filled with people. They were dragged apart, their clothes covered in blood.

'Leave me alone, the rest of you,' said Diaw as he tried to struggle free. 'You think you can lay down the law here, fool. Give thanks to God that I didn't crush you, you swine. And shit to the rest of you!' he yelled vehemently.

He broke free of the restraining hands and rushed up to his room where he double-locked the door and flung himself on the bed. If someone were to ask him why he had got into the fight, he would not have been able to explain. It was the lack of work. A wound had opened up in his heart and he resented everyone while he was living from hand to mouth, even the dockers he had so ardently defended. He wanted to escape, but felt that something was holding him back. And he resented the idle who, without having to raise a finger, lived better than those who had to get up at the crack of dawn. He was suffocating, festering: the growing tumour was poisoning his whole body.

When a man who has lived peacefully for fifty years suddenly sees this happy existence swept away by anguish and disaster, at first he is dumbfounded, and that is the first stage of despair.

That was the case for Lazare, who had spent his whole life building his fortune. His only daughter dead, his wife in prison, he wandered from country to country, constantly changing scene in the hope of curing his grief. In four months, he had visited Switzerland, the Italian Riviera and Spain. His wanderings had done nothing but increase his misery. He returned to Marseilles, and as soon as he got back, an idea took root in his mind. Although he knew his native town like the back of his hand, he had never set foot in the black district. And, if the Africans had been taking any notice, they would have seen this withered, elderly man plodding along, wearing a tattered suit with crumpled trousers and scuffed shoes. There were bags under his eyes and his beard was unkempt. True, in this area, they were used to seeing men like that! Time and time again, he studied the façade of the building, looking at the number of the hotel. Civilians and soldiers strutted about, pausing here and there.

Arabs were selling goods from Paris, spreading their wares on the pavement. Ladies of pleasure, heavily made-up, with tight skirts, swayed their hips and flaunted their frills. Under the porch, two prostitutes on duty called out to the passers-by.

'Coming up, grandad? It's five hundred francs,' said the red-head, walking in Lazare's footsteps. He furtively looked around for someone. His pride was wounded.

The girl came close to him, placing her hand with its blood-red nails on his sleeve. Her face was crudely made-up.

'Would you kindly tell me if Monsieur Diaw Falla lives here?'

'Well! Each to his own taste! So, you're not interested in women?' she scoffed. And then, in a raucous voice, she cried:

'Hey! Juliette! Is Diaw there? There's someone who wants to see him.'

She stood in the street talking to the hotel owner who, leaning out of the window, noted the comings and goings of her flock.

'He can rot for all I care. I don't know what he's up to,' she replied, still harbouring a grudge against her tenant.

'Go up, Monsieur, third floor, the door facing you!'

Lazare climbed the worn stairs. There was a thick layer of dust on the bannisters and there were panes missing from the windows. On each floor, papers and garbage were waiting to be collected. There was a 'Do not disturb' notice on Diaw's door. He stood there for a moment, confused. He knocked falteringly, and let his arm drop to his side. Prompted by a sudden urge, he knocked harder. There was no reply. As he began to retrace his steps, Diaw appeared in the doorway.

'Who are you looking for?'

'Monsieur Diaw Falla.'

'Come in,' said Diaw in surprise.

The room was untidy; books were scattered everywhere, even beside the washbasin. The black man drew up a chair, and motioned his guest to be seated. Unflustered, he looked for his socks, which he took out from between the sheets and the blankets. He hastily made his bed and sat on it.

'What do you want of me?'

Their eyes met. Lazare, who did not yet know why he was there, studied the black man, wondering, 'What am I doing here?'. The Senegalese was also wondering, 'What does he want from me?'

'He's no poor man,' thought Diaw looking at him. 'His suit is made of English cloth. Unhappy, yes, but not poor.'

'Don't you recognize me? I'm Edmond Lazare.'

Diaw racked his brains, trying in vain to remember him.

'Perhaps we've met, but I can't place you. I have a very bad memory of names, and I don't recall your face.'

At these words, the visitor's heart bled. He felt humiliated by this African.

'And yet my name ought to ring a bell. It's not really you I should be seeing but your friend Paul Sonko who's sailing the Pacific Ocean at the moment.'

Diaw was amazed. This man seemed to know Paul and him so well. He was intrigued. He could not remember him. He thought: 'If my memory wasn't so bad, if I had only spoken to him even once ... what the hell does he want from me?'

'Why do you want to see me?'

'I'm Andrée's father.'

'Andrée who d...'

He did not finish his sentence, pointing his index finger.

A suffocating silence followed. Neither dared break it. Although Diaw was stunned, he slowly came round. He recalled the last conversation he had had with the Bambara. He rose, went over to the window and opened it. The room was filled with the clamour of voices.

'Who gave you my address?' he asked angrily.

'I got it from a friend in the police.'

'Forget it!' he cried, irritated by the mention of the police. 'What do you think we are? We're not hooligans, you don't have to go to the cops. To find out what? I read about the affair, you're not to blame. Of course, you have your cross to bear. Your wife acted in the interest of what she calls your reputation. What have you got left? The Way of the Cross.'

Diaw fell silent. He puffed out his chest. Lazare turned his back on him, racked with grief. He remained tongue-tied.

Diaw would have continued treating him harshly if he had not noticed he was crying. He returned to the bed and looked him in the eyes. Speaking more gently he said, 'Why are you crying? It's too late for that. You need courage to face this ordeal,' he advised. 'I met your daughter several times.'

The white man's expression lit up with a feverish joy. That was what he wanted, to hear about his 'Dédée'. He would never tire of talking about her. This transformation did not escape Diaw who, seeing that he could be of use, spoke calmly.

'She was the same age as me. Paul was older than us. We talked about art, feelings, books. Once, yes, I remember, she said to me, "I'll introduce you to my father, you'll see what a good man he is." She was very fond of you. I have a book here, it was she who lent it to me. When I wanted to return it to her, she added, "It's for your birthday." Nobody had ever given me a present before. The last time I saw her ... ah! she was apprehensive about ... I don't know what ... a nice girl! She and Paul came to see me off at the station.'

'You see how kind she was!' said Lazare with tears of relief. 'She was my whole life, I worked only for her, I gave her everything, no sacrifice was too great. I'd rather have seen her bedridden for life than ... dead. It's not possible!'

'Don't cry!' consoled Diaw, feeling the sobs welling up in his throat.

'I feel as if I'm going mad, everything is spinning around me. What's left for me? To wait for death? The tragedy has shattered me so much that I'm losing my memory.'

'Killing yourself is no solution. Only you, and you alone, can understand yourself. Think of your wife. She must need you at the moment, and I'm sure she's sorry for what she did.'

'What about your friend Paul?'

'He holds it against you. Perhaps the sea air will change him. There are memories that are like indestructible ruins. The older they become, the more beautiful they seem.'

'What can I do?'

'Don't let yourself be defeated, recover your faith, if you ever had any. It's good to hope, even if you can no longer count on anything.'

It was a relief for Lazare to hear these words. He took the docker's hand in his by way of thanks.

'My door will never be closed to either you or your friend.'

'Thank you. I'll write to him this evening to tell him of your visit. It is a pity that you can't speak to him.'

'It's not my fault,' said Edmond, shrugging off his responsibility. 'Do you not think I'm suffering enough as it is? In any case, I'm glad to have met you.'

He rose to leave. Diaw saw him down to the next landing and ran back up to his room to lean out of the window.

'How long will he hold out?' mused Diaw.

Diaw had found work thanks to Pipo, replacing someone who had been injured. In the new firm where he was employed, both men and machines had the same orders: to double productivity.

They carried hundred of tonnes on their backs, their arms hurt from the work and their brains throbbed. They all had fits of giddiness and depression from overwork – the infernal pace, the acceleration of the machine. These human robots threw caution to the wind. A worker fell to the bottom of a hold, fracturing his spine. The man had worked a double shift in that hell. In twenty-four hours he had had only four hours' rest.

Falla noted that in general, accidents happened an hour after starting work again, or an hour before work stopped. He himself was exhausted. The docks certainly deserved their nickname of 'man killer'.

The first buds of spring were burgeoning in their thousands. The acacias on the boulevards were covered once more in green foliage which was already coated with grey dust. There was a cheerfulness in the air, and the *pétanque* players were out in force in the warm spring sun.

At the Joliette, the freshly-painted multicoloured little chalets caught the eye. At all hours of the day, the quayside workers, the people from the port and sometimes tourists, came to have lunch there. The damp, dank odour of winter had given way to the good smell of frying.

Since his return from Paris, Diaw had only received two letters. He was waiting for his holiday to find out how Ginette had fared with his book. He groused about his discontent; her behaviour boded no good.

François Sène's family lived in a furnished flat in the place Jules Guesde. His wife, Blanche, had been aptly named – her skin was so pale that the veins in her hands and at her temples showed through. Her arms akimbo, she surveyed her parade ground – four metres by five, which had been invaded by two beds, a wardrobe, the cradle and the kitchen range. All that left her with only a limited space of one square metre. Shortly, eight people were to assemble in this area. She moved the table a second time. Still not satisfied, she vigorously pushed it away, grumbling:

'My God. My God, what on earth made him invite them all

here? Boudiou, it wouldn't matter if it was just the others, but "he" is coming too.'

She pushed a rebel lock of hair back into place. Her face was thickset, as was the rest of her physique. Still complaining, she went over to the cooking pot and examined the contents, an operation that had been repeated numerous times since the beginning of the rearrangement.

'That's it, I've had enough. They'll all squeeze in when they get here.'

The eldest of her three children burst in without her noticing.

'Ma, you'll go barmy if you talk to yourself.'

'There you are. What have you been up to? Go and call Diaw and tell your father to come at once,' ordered the mother.

'Hey!' said the child shaking him, 'are you dead?'

'David,' mumbled Diaw half asleep. 'What's happened?'

'It's time to get up and Ma's waiting for you. I couldn't find Paul, perhaps he's gone off with auntie.'

'What aunt?'

'A real cover girl. She's a bit shy!' replied David leafing through the dictionary.

'Doesn't your mother forbid you to talk like that?'

'What! I'm a man,' announced the child. Turning to Diaw, he went on, 'You're as thin as a rake and you fight the big guys. I don't understand.'

'Will you shut up? Go on, scram, we're leaving.'

Juliette stood outside the office and watched them go. David was tugging at the man's sleeve, and when they were outside, he said, 'Did you see the way that witch ogled you? A right nobody. Aren't you afraid her bloke'll do you in?'

'Tell me, is that the language they teach you at school?'

'What! I'm a man,' repeated the child, shrugging his shoulders. 'I want to be a boxer. You'll teach me to box. You beat up N'Gor, he's a hefty fellow. There's a big boy who's always calling me a nigger, I'd like to punch his face in.'

'You've got the right idea!'

'I ...' interrupted the young Sène, '... look at the old man. All he can do is play poker. The other day, if Ma hadn't stopped me, I'd have kicked him out.'

'What can I say? That's the best school.'

'What do you mean, the best school?'

'Your education has already been completed, in a way.'

'What about you? Why did you leave home? You're not a sailor like them, are you?'

Diaw was surprised at his response and his tone. At a loss for words, he preferred to hold his tongue. He gazed at the boy's frizzy hair and dark skin. They went past a sweet shop.

'Come on, I'll buy you sweets.'

'I don't want any. I'd rather you gave him the dough to go to the flicks.'

He gave him the money. The boy pocketed it hastily and replied, 'Not a word to Ma ... let's keep it to ourselves. You understand? I'll tell her once the money's been spent.'

'I don't see the point in mentioning it afterwards.'

François, in his shirt sleeves, finished arranging the room within its limitations.

'Well!' he said on seeing his son and Falla. 'I dropped in to your place twice, in vain.'

'Hello Blanche'. Diaw kissed the wife before answering the husband. 'Yes, I found your note. We've been working all week. I didn't even hear David come in.'

'Where's auntie?' asked the son and heir.

'She's gone out shopping. Go to the grocer's, you'll find her there. Tell her to get me a litre of milk.'

As he went out, he winked at the docker. His mother noticed and he quickly sneaked away.

'Good Lord!' protested Blanche. 'The children of today! Honestly, when you hear him talking with his father, you'd think he was a man.'

'Children grow up quickly nowadays. Poverty makes their minds develop fast.'

'Poverty. You can say that again! The landlady wants to put up the rent. If we leave, no hotel will have us, because of the kids. To think they're building new houses! Don't be in a rush to get married, wait until you have a roof over your head at least. And the brats! I tell you, it takes away your appetite! What'll become of us!'

The door opened and a young girl came in followed by Paul with the youngest daughter.

'My sister, Danny Rets,' Blanche introduced her.

Her hair was tied in a pony tail and her face was dotted with freckles. She had velvety eyelashes. At first she seemed candid and innocent, but her direct gaze belied that impression. She was wearing a pastel dress with a black belt. She shook Diaw's hand.

'Uncle, look at the earrings auntie bought me,' said the little girl.

'Aren't they lovely! Have you said thank you?'

'Yes, I even gave her a kiss, and I'm going to grandma's for the holidays,' she continued eagerly, clambering into the lap of her aunt who was sitting on the bed.

'What do you think of Marseilles?' Diaw asked the young girl.

'I've seen the Château d'If and the Vierge de la Garde.'

'It's a pity I didn't know you were here,' he joked.

'I feel as if I know you, I've heard so much about you: Diaw this and Diaw that.'

'And what do they say about me?'

'Nothing bad. François says you're elusive.'

'It's very flattering to hear people talking about oneself! But no matter what people say, they always exaggerate. Only gullible souls like that. Apparently you're shy, so they tell me?'

'Oh! The rascal, it's David. I bet!' Blanche tailed off.

'Hell! You're either observant or you're not!'

'Oh you! If we listened to you, children would never be scolded.'

'We have to watch over their education, especially nowadays. In towns, it's deteriorating,' said Danny, going back to the subject which was dear to her heart.

Diaw rejoined, 'It's certainly a good cause to defend, Mademoiselle. From stream to river, how many shores caressed, how many obstacles encountered! Sometimes the water becomes cloudy. Its impurity is not only due to the mud, but to all the things that have been thrown into it. What do kids see these days? What do we have to offer them? We are all responsible for their education. We should give them healthy things to satisfy their curiosity, spiritual nourishment, and not this insanity, these books where there's a murder on every page, a "jargon" that distorts their language and these magazines full of photos of vamps. It is not enough to hide such-and-such a thing from them, it only heightens their curiosity. For example, if you are out with a child and they ask, "What are those women doing on the pavement?" you can't answer that they're waiting for a ... a what? And if you pretend you haven't heard, the child will only insist.'

She did not reply but sat there batting her eyelids. Then she made up her mind and answered:

'If I understand you, we need a reform. In the country you don't find the things you see in towns. People are very polite. You don't meet girls like that either.'

'Ma, here's Bouki,' said David. 'Oh! Catherine's here too!'

'I forgot to tell you, I saw her father,' said François.

'We'll be packed in like sardines.'

'The more the merrier.'

'Will you shut up, David!' shouted his mother.

They helped her set the table. The room was so narrow that half the guests had to sit on the beds. The air was filled with the aroma of peanut sauce. Catherine entered, followed by a man.

'You?' burst out Diaw in surprise. 'I wonder what on earth François said to your father?'

'Really!' exclaimed Catherine with a hint of anger in her voice. 'You act so surprised every time he lets me out, anyone would think he was a savage.'

'Heavens, no!'

Bouki, who was the guest of honour, had brought a bunch of flowers and some cakes. His dapple grey suit comprised every colour of the spectrum. He was anxious to preserve his well-earned reputation as a lady-killer. After the introductions, he seated himself between Catherine and Danny. When they were all settled, as comfortably as possible, Blanche passed round the plates of rice and *maffé*.*

'Have you ever eaten African food before?' Bouki asked Danny.

'No!'

'Tell us what you think of it. Your sister cooks it better than a Sudanese woman.'

'You can say that again,' retorted François, who, as a

---

*Chicken peanut stew.

Christian, crossed himself before plunging his spoon into the food.

'It's odd, Cath, even though he's poor, he's a believer. But I don't think the good Lord's much of a mathematician. He can add, multiply and subtract, but he can't divide. He gets confused with the dividends and deductions,' said his wife who stood surveying the others.

'Come here, next to me,' called her husband moving over to make room on the bed. He went on, 'I fell out with the priest yesterday. Would you believe he wants to photograph us for the parish magazine so that he can boast, "Look, there are blacks in the choir." We refused, then he turned round and told us it was a sacrilege. That was going too far! I told him that we are humble believers and we don't come to church for social advancement, unlike the rich members of the parish who only give to charity to get themselves noticed. There are five of us living in a closet ... and these people who come and listen to the sermon, what are they doing about mutual aid?'

'What did he say to that?' asked his wife.

'What do you expect? He wriggled out of it. And yet, he's kind,' he concluded, to make up for getting carried away.

'I'll never understand you. In the morning you go to church, then you go and sign on the dole and then, the bars! What do you ask God for?' said Blanche.

'To let me win at cards so I can feed my family.'

'And when you lose?'

'Then it's up to you!'

François and Diaw nearly choked with laughter. The former laughed so heartily that tears ran down his face. Watching them made everyone else laugh too.

'Why are they laughing, mummy?' asked little Chantal.

'Your father ought to know.'

François was helpless with mirth. He raised his arm to explain, his eyes met Blanche's and he snorted even louder.

'You're stupid, what are you sniggering at?'

'I promise you, it's not you,' said François between two convulsions.

'That's enough!' thumped Catherine firmly.

'Ma! I'm going to the cinema,' announced David once calm had been restored.

'And where did you get the money from? And don't call me Ma any more, call me mummy', she shouted furiously.

'I gave it to him.'

'You spoil that child, Diaw. Everything I refuse him, you let him have. It's all right for today.' And turning to her son, 'Take your sister with you.'

'I want to stay with auntie,' implored the girl.

They finished the meal and the table was rapidly cleared. Diaw lay comfortably on the bed, his feet dangling over the end, his head resting on Catherine's thighs. Bouki acted as Danny's partner. François helped his wife and ground the coffee. A packet of *Chesterfield* was handed round.

'Don't mind us,' said François to the docker.

'I didn't know you were jealous?'

'Huh! Why should I be? By the way, Cath, when's the wedding?'

'If it were up to me ...!' she sighed, heaving her chest.

'You know I have a very broad notion of married life. The only thing I don't like about it is the idea of private property,' said Diaw.

'Are you afraid?'

'No, Danny.'

'Oh yes you are,' she retorted. 'Either you don't feel capable of making her happy, or you don't like yourself.'

'You may be right.'

'Now he's hiding. When he says someone may be right, that's the end of the discussion,' riposted his lady-love, tweaking his hair.

'Ouch!' cried Diaw.

'It's the same with my beau. If you want to get married, stand firm,' added Blanche.

'Holy Mary! That's a bit much!'

'To the devil with you. I'll send you and the children back to Goré. He's ashamed to go to the cinema with me. If it weren't for Diaw, I'd never go out. And you think I'd be sorry to see you go? Oh no I wouldn't. He's afraid of people staring at him and François Sène would like to remain anonymous. He isn't good looking.'

'I agree with you there,' cut in François. 'The other day, as I was on my way home, there were police saying to the tourists, "Don't go into the black district." And yet, nobody gets killed there, women don't get attacked. "Nigger" is synonymous with "mugger". But what about them? They are technical barbarians.'

'What I don't like,' added Bouki, 'is that you say "the black district". Nobody makes the blacks live there. Let people go elsewhere and get attacked, serves them right! Silence is the highest form of disdain.'

'We've got a huge complex,' continued Diaw. 'We're quite happy to look at a Chinese person, or an Indian, but if they look at us, we shrink to nothing. A glance does no harm. Suffering has always attracted attention.'

'Are you mad? Do you have to lose your marbles too? Blacks this and blacks that. I'm getting fed up with it. And what are we supposed to do?' asked François bitterly.

'And yet, they ought to be used to you. There's no shortage of your fellow countrymen around here.'

'Indeed, Mademoiselle,' said Bouki who was standing drinking his coffee. He went on: 'All that is partly our fault and partly their idiocy.'

'Perhaps, but if a girl goes out with a black man, she's ostracized.'

'I wouldn't go that far,' said Diaw. 'There's Cath's father who doesn't want me for a son-in-law even though he and I are of the same race. What father doesn't try to stand in the way of his daughter's choice? I'm not blaming anyone – people are stupid. It's a weary and petty world. It's dangerous to have the world against you. A young girl's reputation is a very fragile thing, even more so than her honesty. It's easy to cast a slur on her character. Words and deeds are misinterpreted through narrow-mindedness, spite and lack of indulgence, but mostly through lack of intelligence. Yes, this world is weary and petty. And yet we have to break out of this dogma of ignorance.'

'Here's your milk,' said Blanche.

Catherine held the glass. She too was satisfied.

'I have to bow to the evidence. It's three against one,' declared Danny.

'What do you think of the police who demand your papers

when you're with someone? I feel as though I'm on the scrap-heap. They treat us as if we're the dregs of society.'

'Oh! Don't torment yourself, Bouki! What happened to you could have happened to anyone. Why take it out on everyone?'

A long silence set in. It was as though nobody dared speak. The two children were asleep. Danny lay her niece down behind Bouki and went back to her chair with her back to the window. As nobody broke the ice, she said:

'Do you prefer to abandon your ancestral customs and adopt those of Europe or what?'

'As far as I know, there is nothing wrong with our customs,' replied Bouki. 'Some of our rites could be abolished, I agree, but our dances are a whole culture. Nudity isn't savageness, but purely a question of acclimatization. Of course, sometimes it's pleasanter to have a squint at someone who's come from the tailor's than someone parading around in their birthday suit. Only clothes develop an insatiable need in them which pushes them to wild vices. And often, to keep up-to-date, they act in a shameful fashion. Here, respect is a matter of one's get-up.'

'Well said, Bouki,' contributed Diaw, 'yet, can you explain to me what a civilization is, Danny?'

Danny remained silent, at a loss for words.

'I pity you, love, you're caught between two fires. They've never spent so long in this room,' said Blanche.

'Each continent has its own,' began François. 'When my Father lies around in the sun exposing his stomach, seen through the eyes of the *toubabs*, he's a savage, at least in appearance. Yet from his own kind, he receives the honours due to his rank, he keeps to the customs. If my mother walks barefoot, if the soles of her feet spread, I don't see why that makes her inferior. To the European, a well-dressed black is someone who has adapted to their way of life, as if the Negro came from another planet.'

'Yes,' agreed Diaw, 'and you yourself know nothing of black people other than what you've read in books.'

'It's true!' admitted Danny.

'So you asked that question out of curiosity. Not that I blame you, but I blame your ancestors who crammed your head full of nonsense about our behaviour. But if a black person says something sensible, or reasonably sensible, you're surprised. So you have two conflicting pictures, the one inherited from your ancestors and the one you have within your grasp. Sometimes I hear people say, "Oh! He isn't like the rest of them." What strikes them, is that it's a black person saying it, for they didn't expect anything from him.

'The thing is, we can understand you. But you can't understand us. I think that should satisfy you,' concluded Diaw mockingly.

'I apologize for asking such an idiotic question. On my way here, I bought a book which won the Grand Prix for Literature this year, by the way. It's on slavery.'

'Well, well,' said the docker. 'I've written something like that too.'

'It's by Ginette Tontisane.'

'What did you say?' bellowed Diaw as if he had not heard. He sat down.

'I've got it here. I can show it to you.'

While she rummaged in her bag, the room was silent. The rumble of the traffic and the sounds from the street filled the air. Diaw watched the girl impatiently. His heart was racing. He began to perspire.

'Here you are,' said Danny, handing him the book.

'Is it the one you wrote?' asked Catherine.

'Yes,' he replied.

He rushed out, slamming the door.

'What's he going to do?' asked Danny.

'He doesn't know himself. He's going to shut himslf up in his room,' replied François.

Diaw was a man who quivered at the slightest touch and who, once he got carried away, was capable of anything. He had an iron will: the hurdles he encountered did not discourage him. He was first and foremost a sportsman and he despised cheating of any sort. When he dug his heels in, he expected to come out on top. The same day he learned of Ginette's treachery, he left Marseilles for Paris. There had been a mistake, and he had to have an explanation.

He went to the novelist's apartment twice during the day without being able to see her. That evening, he visited the cellar clubs of Saint-Germain-des-Prés where daytime celebrities finished off their nights. He found her, very late, at the Pergola, seated at a table with two companions. He stared at her. Her hair was bleached and she was heavily made up. She was talking animatedly. He said nothing to her but returned to wait on her doorstep, without giving vent to his anger.

'Ah!' exclaimed the woman as the black man's hand clamped down over her mouth to prevent her from screaming.

'Open the door,' he ordered.

They entered a lavishly-furnished apartment. The polished parquet floor shone. He closed the door and gave Ginette a violent shove.

She said, 'I wrote to tell you there had been a mistake, but the letter came back to me!'

He had to restrain himself from going for her throat. His blazing eyes expressed the passion raging within him. His nails dug deep into the palms of his clenched fists. He did not want to give way to the violence inside him. She drew closer to him.

'For Christ's sake! You've got the better of me twice, and now you're trying to turn on the charm. What do you take me for? A blackmailer or your gigolo?'

'Hold on a minute, let me explain!'

Like a wild animal, he sprang, crushing her arm. With his other hand, he thrust her head down.

'You're hurting me,' she moaned.

'You hurt me a lot more.'

He pushed her on to the corner divan. He was beside himself, seized by an uncontrollable rage.

'Do you know what it's like to live from hand to mouth? To live in a hovel? To work like the nigger I am? To sell my clothes because I can't pay the rent? To get up at dawn and return home in the evening exhausted, drained, spent? No. I doubt you know what it's like. Do you know that you have also robbed another woman?

'Me?'

'Yes, you,' he said sarcastically, sitting down. 'You have robbed Catherine. She was counting on that book for us to be able to get married. She was banking on it. It was her dream, the hopes of a young girl.'

He lowered his voice, 'She's pregnant. Do you realise what you've done? You've destroyed everything. You took me for a "nigger".

He had ended up uttering it. For him, 'nigger' meant ignorant, rough, foolish. It was more than a struggle between the robber and the robbed. Two races stood face to face, centuries of hatred confronted each other.

'I'll give you money, and I'll send you more. I'm not to blame.'

'Of course you're not, I am! Do you think I'm that stupid? The minute I'm out of here, you'll phone the police. There are things that can neither be bought nor sold. You've made your name through my work, through my suffering.

'Earlier on, you recognized me, didn't you? But I was an embarrassment. You're anxious to protect your new reputation!'

He twisted her arm again. His hands felt like lead gripping her painful limb.

'Let me go. I'll give you everything I've got.'

They stood up. She tried to jerk herself free from his grasp.

'Careful, you'll hurt yourself,' advised Diaw.

She obeyed, white-faced. She took a bundle of notes from the table drawer. He snatched them with his free hand.

'It's incredible what you bourgeois think you can do with money! Do you think that's why I'm here?'

'Take it, I'll give you more, I swear I will. Have you forgotten the time we spent together?'

'Who cares!' he cried. 'I've already told you, you won't get round me with charm. My word, you take me for a pimp!' His grip tightened. She moaned as if caught in a stranglehold. He felt no pleasure in what he was doing, but he had to humiliate her. Then suddenly, he let go. Released, she panted, choking. Her shoulder blade was so painful that she could not move it.

He looked at her, gazing at her with hatred, biting his lips until he drew blood. He tried to control his anger. Unable to contain himself, he flew at her. Her head banged against the corner of a piece of furniture, she collapsed. Seeing her lying on the floor, he left.

After the drama, Diaw wandered along the banks of the Seine, deep in thought. How long had he been sitting there? He had not the faintest idea. His head in his hands, he said over and over again: 'It's not possible, she can't be dead.' The newspaper he was holding gave an account of the murder. He was flabbergasted, he could not understand what was happening to him.

He went to the Gare de Lyon, too weak to stand up, and sank on to a bench. He needed to relieve himself but even that decision was beyond him. His limbs were overcome with a great weariness.

He was sleepy, but how could he sleep with the law after him? He had to defend himself, but against whom, and how? His intelligence forced him to collect his wits. His thoughts were soon swept away by fear, an icy fear. Then he was overcome with hatred, against all those who were a different colour from him. His head was buzzing like a swarm of bees. He was suddenly overwhelmed by a violent surge of anger. He hunched himself up, muttering under his breath, repeating over and over again that he was a murderer, that he was outlawed from society because he was black. Everything was a result of that word.

His pride as a black, and his pride as a man dictated his actions. He jumped to his feet and made an effort to consider himself like the other people who were coming and going. As he watched them, he wondered whether anybody else was experiencing the same feelings and the same anguish as he was. He walked past a police officer without looking up from the newspaper he was pretending to read. This new feeling of his value as a human being guided his steps, and even helped him board the train. He had no idea what the time was or when the train left. He was glad to find himself alone in the compartment. The dull glow from the light on the platform shone into his face. He jerked down the blind.

He tried to analyse what was going on inside him. He could dissect the days, the years and the centuries and still never find what he wanted to know. It was something to do with class, wealth, the strong and the weak. It had never occurred to him before that one day he would be a criminal. 'And why?' he asked himself. He could not admit that he had become a killer. Ginette's death had completely destroyed him. He could see no way out, his thoughts raced and clanged inside his head.

The carriage rattled. A passenger had opened the door and closed it again on meeting his eyes. Happy in his solitude, he stretched out on the seat, allowing himself to be lulled by the monotonous sound of the engine starting up. He could not rid himself of his obsession.

He had been shut up in his room for five days. It was like a prison cell. This cubby-hole had taken on, in his eyes, a priceless value. It was a vast land where all sorts of flowers bloomed and countless birds fluttered. This hovel seemed more welcoming than a castle full of precious objects. He did not have much time left in which to enjoy life like this, he was a murderer, a 'nigger murderer' he said to himself.

When the door opened, he jumped, his pulse beat twice as fast. The light was switched on. Catherine stood before him, holding his food. He stared at the girl for a long time. Her stomach was growing round. The blood rushed to his eyes.

'Why don't you leave. I'll be with you!'

She was ready to sacrifice everything for her love. Receiving no response, she knelt down and took the man's head in her hands. Diaw Falla felt a great surge of relief at her touch. She tightened her embrace and said:

'If only I could crush it for you, just to see what was inside! Even then, I wouldn't have got much further. Good Lord, you didn't kill her, they say she fell after an argument. Oh! Tell me what's tormenting you. It's not enough that she robbed you, I have to lose you as well. No, I'd rather die.'

'Don't say that!'

They were silent. She buried her head in the hollow of his shoulder. He fearfully looked up into her eyes. What he wanted to tell her was stronger than what he kept repeating to himself when he was alone. His feverishness prevented him from speaking. He sat devastated in his silence. He found it was even stupid and useless to speak, to open his mouth. And yet, he forced out the impulses constricting his throat.

'Don't worry,' he began, in a softer voice. 'I aimed too high, and here I am, lower than the ground. What have I got to hope for now? They'll come. You're a good, kind girl. As I told you, I've written to my uncle about you and the child. I've understood my mistake, and it's too late!'

'Don't give up! You must fight!'

'What's the use?'

His breath came in slow convulsions. He broke free from her and rose. He paced up and down the room. The woman's presence was a reminder of the torch of freedom. He drank some water, it had a bitter taste, but it did his knotted stomach good. Prompted by the urge to speak, his heart swelled.

'I know you're getting into a state, all I've brought you is unhappiness and trouble. I don't want you to forget me. It'll be nice for me in ... ' – he was afraid to say prison and changed the subject – 'I don't want you mixed up in all this. I must pay for my mistake on my own.'

'What about me? What'll become of me? And what about the child, have you thought about him? When my father finds out, he's capable of killing me. Perhaps that'd be for the best! Don't give up, you've got to defend yourself and me! Where's your old strength? You're everything to me, you're all I've ever known.'

Catherine studied him. She was ready to do anything. She went to his side and placed her hand on Diaw's shoulder. He did not understand what she wanted in touching him. She loved him, and wanted to prove it to him. But the gulf that separated them was as vast as that between the heaven and earth. They were as different as day and night. The man unfastened the chain which he never removed from his neck and from which hung two tiny horns, and gave it to her, saying:

'Here you are, you've always wanted it. Keep it, and if there are times when you feel sad, shake them for me. Now go home.'

'No, I'm staying.'

'Not now. Besides, everything in its own good time. You see, I no longer have the right to do anything, except wait.'

'I want to wait with you,' she said, clinging to him.

His thoughts were muddled. When she was there, he found it impossible to think clearly. The bitterness of his act was a sweet gall compared to that in his heart. He shook his head to stop himself from breaking down in front of her.

'You mustn't stay here,' he said, pushing her towards the door.

She clutched him, sobbing. Every heave of her breast was a knife through him. He did not want to give in. He saw her out and slammed the door.

'Diaw! Diaw!' she called from the other side.

He took his head in his hands. He was utterly exhausted, his mind was numb and his body no longer responded to any stimuli. He slid down against the door and crumpled to the floor. The next day, he was still in the same position when he was arrested.

'I'm optimistic,' said Riou, rubbing his hands, 'they've been deliberating for over an hour now. No doubt they'll rule out premeditation.'

'Will they?' replied Diaw, coming out of his torpor.

A few moments later, he was taken into the courtroom. The judge invited him to stand. The noise had suddenly abated. Then the judge read out the verdict:

'To the first question, "Is the defendant capable of having deliberately killed Ginette Tontisane?" the majority of the jury replied "yes".

'To the second question, "Was there premeditation?" the majority of the jury replied "yes".

'To the third question, "Can the defendant plead mitigating circumstances?" the majority of the jury replied "yes".

'Consequently, in accordance with articles 302 and 463 of the Penal Code, Diaw Fallas is sentenced to life imprisonment. The prisoner has three clear days to take his case to the Court of Appeal.'

The journalists now rushed towards him. He watched them, distraught, these men no longer looked the same to him as before.

PART III

THE LETTER

... Prison, 195...

Dear Uncle,

You are probably wondering whether I am still alive. Life has no meaning for me. I hestitated for months and months before writing these lines to you: finally, my urge to do so got the better of me. How can I not write when I have so much time at my disposal as I await death? Do not think that I am complaining ... Anyway, to whom would I complain, and what would be the point?

Here I am, following what could be called the course of destiny. For three hundred and sixty-five days, I was haunted by a single thought. To better grasp it, I let another year go by. In the past, when I was a member of society, I believed I was just a man like everybody else. I could think as I pleased. But now, I am the slave of my own thoughts. Society holds my body captive; one thought imprisons my mind, there is nothing but this relentless obsession: that I must live here until my death, between four cold bare walls, with no surface or horizon where my gaze can rove. My eyes can offer me nothing but this prospect of humility. In my cell, only my imagination, where the real merges with the imaginary, gives me the illusion of escape.

Whatever I think, my thoughts always hark back to my obsession – THAT I WILL DIE HERE.

I wonder when and how death will come to me? Hugo said that man is sentenced to death with an indefinite reprieve. So what next? Why don't I rejoice? Why this obsession? What have I got to lose? The dark, monotonous days, the icy, damp nights, the badly-cooked bread, my meagre portion of broth, a mixture of refuse and scraps? Sometimes I'm pleased I didn't appeal. The director says that, depending on my good conduct, I'll earn certain concessions, such as a shortening of my sentence which, he says, will reduce my stay in this castle to twenty or thirty years. I'm well over twenty-four years old. Work it out. In which Year of Grace will I be released?

I have no illusions as to their leniency. I am riveted here, I must DIE here. Well, they'd better not trouble me about my conduct. Even if I were an exemplary prisoner, how long would I have left to sample life? I would not be able to see my loved ones again. My mother is dead, the sentence killed her. Poor mother, how she must have suffered! Catherine has left her father. She is prostituting herself to keep our son. It would have been possible to save her, but she has sunk to the depths. She has taken to the bottle and risks going mad. Apparently, when a person is in that state of mind, the brain deteriorates and they do not think very much. Sometimes, I hope it will happen to her. Talking of madness, sometimes my own mind goes blank.

The child bears my name.

He came into the world as I was removed from it. He will do his military service when I will be leaving feet first. Diaw Falla junior will soon be three years old. What will be his future? This is what I would like for you, my child, since I shall no longer enjoy these things: sunshine, spring, flower-filled meadows, birds that wake you with their chirping, trees, nature, and, above all, freedom. But respect humankind, avoid wounding its dignity. Let your arguments be fair. Let the pure expression of your feelings not be marred by the greed for fortune. Those are the fundamental necessities of life, they are its essence. Love life with all your soul, do not lose your heart in the debauchery of this century.

I am not serving my sentence. I am banished from society. My mother is no longer. Her age? I don't remember exactly, fifty or sixty. In any case, her death was hastened by my conviction. My wife, if I can call her that, paces up and down the street like a sentry. This work, which goes against morality, which novelists and films decry, is repulsive. Who knows, she might end up under the protection of a procurer?

Then what will become of my son? This child, who smiles happily in his sleep, who thinks of nothing? It's the thought of him that hurts me. I am an orphan, Cath a widow, the child half abandoned, the three of us are victims of an act of law. No wonder my nights are haunted. What difference will it make to me whether I die today or tomorrow? Bash my head against the wall? What's the point? Having thought about it, I won't give in, for I don't want to give those who shut me away here the satisfaction of seeing me die as they predicted. For me, death will be a deliverance, I await it like a lover pining for his 'belle'.

I will go to meet it with outstretched arms. I will utter just two words: 'Thank you'. I do not imagine you will share my ideas, death is a spectre one does not easily embrace. For me, it will be natural.

Your letter, which I have just received, made me lose track of my ideas. You can write to me every day, but I can only write once a month. Perhaps they are afraid I'll get carried away?

Wretched laws and wretched men, I am not bad. In my more lucid moments, when I feverishly collect my thoughts, I think of the charge, not the crime, and I feel more remorse than before I was sentenced. I no longer have room for anything other than DEATH. So why don't they curtail this life?

They certainly apply the law. It is not enough to make a plaster cast, they must also dissect and carry out the intellectual autopsy of a defendant. At what precise moment did I commit the crime? They refer to the date and the time. What was my state of mind? To find the answer, they take me to a psychiatrist. They will even give me sweets to calm me down. Hell! When I'm clear-headed, I would no sooner harm a flower than I would a human being!

The doctor came, or rather, I went to see him. He's the prison doctor. Recently, an inmate hanged himself. They tried in vain to revive him. On another occasion, it was Mathieu who slashed his wrists. Apparently, he's been here for twelve years. Both were convinced they would not be pardoned.

To get back to the doctor, he told me I was in good health and gave me some pills for my insomnia. When I told him that I was young, that my blood ran freely in my veins and that I was suffering from a man-made illness, he answered that that was outside his field and that I'd do better to consult a priest. I went to the chapel to find him.

We prisoners really are spoiled by the taxpayers – in short, well, never mind. I was disappointed in my quest. His lordship the priest was in town. It is his vocation to be here, prisoner of his ideas! One fine morning – if I use the word fine, it's merely a turn of phrase, there is nothing here I can describe as such – the priest came. He stood there in front of me. For lack of a chair, I invited him to sit on my bed. Oh! he didn't decline, even though I wished he had. He's here to help us, to share our sorrow. Now there's a misunderstanding. He began by asking me if I believed in God. I interrupted him saying that I had no business with God. Is he keeping me in this place? Why turn to him when it is men who are hurting you? That killed the conversation. Much as I longed for company, his got on my nerves. Yes, low as I have sunk, I am neither an atheist nor ungodly. God is my witness. But what did this priest say that was heartfelt, kind or resounding? He wrung nothing from my heart, not even a pang. Of course, you'll say, I am no more a Christian than I am a Muslim. I was expecting to hear from his lips words that would bring tears to my eyes. He honoured me with Latin quotations. Does a negro need this language? Are we to understand that the Almighty speaks only one tongue? He recites litanies parrot-fashion, pieces that are graven in his mind. He chants them with ease, without even a frown clouding his silly face. I respect him because of his cassock. Jesus would have understood me. He suffered through man and for man. Far be it for me, however, to compare myself to him!

At recreation – because I don't want to work, and for good reason – I see the priest giving advice to the others.

'He's a good chap,' a fellow inmate tells me.

So, I'm the bad one, as is borne out by the documents – for it's society that makes men what they are!

A few days later, I was cleaning my tomb, as hygiene requires, when I heard the bolts grate back, and who should be standing there? His lordship the priest! I immediately said that God must like black, since he always wore that colour. He pretended not to have heard. Then he conversed with me about my book and about my past. But he knows nothing about my future. Then we came to speak of belief. He's a good theologian. He would like to go and teach in Africa. He ruined everything by saying that. No, God isn't a cover that can be transported anywhere, he isn't only to be found in one country. When I began to talk about slavery, he seemed to be struck by ... I don't know what. He left. Whew! I've got rid of him for a few days. I don't know why I annoyed him. It wasn't intentional. With this prickling in my head, I don't know anything any more.

How long have I been here? Stupid question, sinister idea. How could it have formed inside me?

After my conversation with the chaplain, I remained as if petrified by indecision.

I have not once thought of Africa, and now she appears to me in all her beauty, drenched with air and sunshine, and it is impossible for me to think of anything else.

Yes, as I've already said, prison kills everything. It is something vile and loathsome with its unhealthiness, its venom which withers everything, its bitter gall. It is a leech preying on the soul, it neither contains nor combats offences, it exacerbates and expands them, and you are condemned for the rest of your life.

Before the verdict, when the judge asked me if I had anything to say, I was short of breath and I heard a voice say: 'Ask why you killed.' They wouldn't have been capable of giving me an explanation.

I have learned a language which is not my own. At school, they told me about the goodness of a city and when I came to this country, to live, I had to work. I stumbled under the weight of my load. Every evening I returned home broken, worn out from exhaustion, for days, weeks and years on end. At night, I wrote. To get this book published, I entrusted it to a woman, she stole from me, and then humiliated me. She made a name for herself from my work. All these facts are simply theories of provocation, neglected by the law. You saw the charge. Why didn't you try to understand what aroused my anger and prompted this crime which I refuse to recognize? I am black!

I could have got myself killed in the war, or paraded along the Champ-Elysées, puffing out my chest. I could have been a servant for someone like you – why not? You would have granted me one evening off per week, just to give your 'nigger' a break.

I recall a piece I had to learn by heart at school:

'The loyalty of the Senegalese infantrymen to their leaders is admirable.
These good people are completely devoted to their commander.'

I'm abridging it (memory failure).

'The officer cannot forget the look
in the eyes of these men who fall
never to rise again. They are proper
French soldiers.
We cannot employ them otherwise
than in the service of the Fatherland.'

There's clear teaching for you! My father never broke the law. He respected the individual, avoided doing anyone any moral damage, thus obeying 'human' laws. And yet, as he was unable to read or write, he could not have been a member of a jury!

The legal system can sometimes create criminals: rights of scoundrels, reasoning of donkeys.

When I was in detention, before being transferred to this prison, I watched young delinquents turn into habitual offenders. The law has only one remedy: isolate them. For the men of law, they are plague-stricken and it is better to house them in this lazaret. How are they treated here? Prison is no more a sedative than it is a specific remedy.

You are at the bedside of a dying man. The illness interests you less than the patient. The diseased member can no longer be saved. You decide to amputate. Good, saved, you say, but the next day, it's a different part of the body that is affected, in a different way – and so on until there's nothing left. With this solution, it's the patient who dies. It is the same with the adolescents you lock up. No, you do not cure them. You temporarily appease their sickness. When they come out, on contact with society, they become habitual offenders, the virus is within you, in everything that surrounds you.

These days, punishment goes against the evidence. The old windmill which comprises the book of codes and decrees has broken down. It is common for people to say: 'In my day this, in my day that', 'If you aren't capable of doing it, get out'. Stop saying that the young are perverted. Isn't the very fabric of society paralysed by vice?

It is even more absurd to say that evil is not a product of the times. Where do murders, abortions, poisoning, theft, prostitution, alcoholism and homosexuality come from? From unemployment! There are too many unemployed! An accumulation of poverty: that is the root of all evil. Is it the churches or the leaders who are no longer at the service of the people? Whatever the reason, the masses are dying.

So refuse to allow yourselves to be ruled by those who are only concerned with their own interests. The working class is too poor, young people are reduced to begging, with no fire or spiritual nourishment.

In Africa, there are too many ignorant, too many sick. It is the fault of the institutions. All those people without bread, without joy, the only thing they are rich in is poverty. The scales are tipped in favour of a 'handful of men' who have everything.

There are too many people who spend their time shouting, exchanging insults, making decrees, getting bogged down in various questions relating to the betterment of the people – goodness knows what they're trying to do. They extend their overtime at our expense, to make amendments and bellow. Between futile quarrels, they collect votes of confidence, go from opposition to opposition, from ministerial collapse to ministerial collapse. Whether they belong to the extremes or to the centre of the government, they call themselves names which are totally incompatible with their ideal, and it is the people that suffer.

Tell them to step outside their Houses of Parliament. Let each one go to his constituency to consult his voters, to see the homes of the delinquents, the unemployed, the old people and abandoned children. Then, in the evening, by way of distraction, let them go and inspect the streets under the protection of the vice squad. Then they'll see that there's no point in prolonging their vigil. They will also find out that loans, charity, national children's days and things like that are not solutions. They lead nowhere because it is always the poor who give. Let them go down among the people and start reforms. They should not be afraid of getting themselves dirty in the hovels. Then let them dismantle the old windmill of the law and revise the penal code. Re-educate the politicians and the judges, build schools, bring all that into line with the present. The past dictates nothing. These people are too numerous and are too great a burden on the economy. They know too much to govern, but not enough to deliver us from poverty, and that is what jeopardizes everything. They are responsible for the vices of both sexes, likewise for all their misdeeds. Science has produced wonders. The splitting of the atom disturbs and terrifies you, and you think this will be the salvation of mankind? You are wrong! In continuing this research, you will end up worshipping your machines. Then you will be nothing but mascots trying to catch up with yourselves. Conscience will remain the unexploited phenomenon. You will quarrel over vast areas, forgetting how many feet you need for your own graves. A single movement of the earth, a fragment of thunder will annihilate you. Each person is a plant in the garden of humanity, cultivate it, water it with moral standards, tend it. Tomorrow it will provide you with excellent shelter, fertile in kindness, and the twilight of existence will find you united. There, uncle, my first and last letter. I have omitted nothing. I have aged a lot during this short time. I witness every movement, I hear the commotion of life. Alone, and at a distance, the soul rises to the surface and bathes in the waters of solitude.

Here, everything seems crystal clear to me! You can never see what is right in front of your eyes. My body may be suffering discomfort, but my soul is at rest. Everything in me seems void. When I think of God, I become so minute that my tears, which I thought had dried up for ever, well up from the depths of my emotions.

I have seen more than my years but I have lived only one spring.

I shall not say goodbye, or so long.

We shall meet in God.

DIAW FALLA